# IMPOSSIBLE LIVES
# OF
# BASHER THOMAS
*a novel*

Robert Detman

*For my parents*

FIRST FIGUREGROUND PRESS EDITION, NOVEMBER, 2014

*Copyright © 2014 by Robert Mark Detman*

All rights reserved. Published in the United States by Figureground Press, a division of Innocents and Infidels, in 2014.

This is a work of fiction. Any resemblance to figures either living or dead is purely a coincidence, and cannot be construed as intentional or useful in any context outside of the world of *Impossible Lives of Basher Thomas*.

Portions of this novel have appeared as: "First Time, Last Time", *Akashic Books Thursdaze*, September, 2014; "The Watch", in *Driftwood: A Literary Journal of Voices from Afar*, Vol. 2, No. 2, Fall, 2008, in altered form. An earlier version of "The Watch" first appeared as "Harry Obscured" in *The Pitkin Review*, Fall 2004.

ISBN-13: 978-0692243497
ISBN-10: 0692243496

Cover photograph by Getty Images/Sisoje

figuregroundpress.org

ROBERT DETMAN

# IMPOSSIBLE LIVES OF BASHER THOMAS

Robert Detman has published fiction in the *Antioch Review, Akashic Books, Santa Monica Review* and numerous other literary journals. His short story collection, *The Survivor's Guide*, was a semi-finalist for *The Hudson Prize* from *Black Lawrence Press* in 2013. A graduate of The University of Michigan, he has a Master of Fine Arts in Creative Writing from Goddard College.

robertmdetman.com

# IMPOSSIBLE LIVES
# OF
# BASHER THOMAS

*a novel*

ROBERT DETMAN

# I. ARTIFACT

Film slowed to one sixteenth speed. He moves his mouth as if to speak or take a breath. Eyebrows rise up in query. Hands turn palm up to display acquiescence. Head rises with eyebrows rise and drops again. Head making nodding motion, easy, almost unconcerned. Nodding increasing, with mild emphasis, a flicker of concern. Hand goes to forehead and brushes hair to side. Hand scratches temple. Look more concerned. Mouth forms words with teeth showing. Lips moving balletic through enunciation. Eyes squint and head turns at angle to see more clearly. Hands go up at sides and palms now face forward as if the desire to catch oneself in a fall. Distorted sound on tape like a pucker or a wave landing on a beach. Five more in succession. Arm that scratched temple now thrust forward to meet object. Object streaks into figure as figure jolts back on heels to meet object. Object flutters into shirt of figure and figure falls out of frame. Camera moves to follow figure now on ground gripping the ground. Camera shudders as dropped to low angle and moved in to meet figure.

**December, 1981**

Over rolled cigarettes, two tents loft imperceptibly, illusorily, in the winter dawn. Their talks have a quality where Basher tries to educate Harry in the ways of the sophisticated world he runs around in. Directed as the lessons probably are at Harry's recent anxiety and intending, Harry knew, to provide comfort. Much of it was simply calling up their incidental past.

"Harry, you know that stuff meant a lot to me, right? We were kind of freaked out then, weren't we?"

Harry thinks he understands what Basher means, because it is what he wants it to mean. Rather, that Basher doesn't say, *you* were freaked out, which is what Harry thinks he might say, (and what Harry knows), and instead says *we*, makes a big difference.

The Baja highway is partially paved—and in those stretches it is a narrow two lane barely wide enough for a single vehicle, let alone the trucks that barrel down it all night long. With its sinkholes, craters and chassis wracking vados and deep V dips, the only warning is when the roadway drops from the headlights. Driving Ensenada to San Vicente to Camalu to Colonet to San Quintin to El Rosario to Mulege, and onward, Basher's goal is to cross the Tropic of Cancer for the new year. So that they can spend their precious break on the beach, they drive at night when caravans of semi-trucks carelessly take over the roads. There are numerous cattle, also. Harry closes his eyes in the bright lights that sweep over them.

The winter sky over Baja: Orion stretches wide, spanning what looks like a third of the sky, in mid-cartwheel from the slumbering horizon to the canopy of midnight blue above.

Basher stands up and looks at the sky. He stretches his arms out wide in a kind of self-conscious yogi pose. Pointing, says, "That there, you can almost make them out, are the nebulas: Barnard's loop. A couple million years it's been there, Harry. Maybe billions. You believe that?" Basher reaches down and takes a pinch of the earth between his fingers and snaps it into the air.

"Us? We're dust. Insignificant. But you know what? I don't feel it. Look at that out there. We're part of it, man. We're connected to it. I wanna touch those stars."

Harry wonders at these moments about Basher's sincerity, and tries to see it. Orion. Basher's doppelgänger. Alone. Nothing is in the dark that is not there in the day. Whatever happens to you, happens to me.

Basher's self-certainty overwhelms as much as it fascinates him.

If none of it matters anyway, just like Basher always says, why let anything stop you? Why not go for it? Basher will understand. The troubles he wrestled with—that's what is insignificant. The word repeated in Harry's head until nothing made sense anymore.

*Insignificant, insignificant, insignificant.*

## Document: State Department Report. July, 2002

Status, declassified.

    Name: Nathaniel Lion Thomas {alias "Basher" Thomas.}

    Age: 23 years.

    D.O.D.: August 17, 1982

    Professional Affiliation(s): International Assoc. Press Bureau (Paris)

    Action: Decease by Firearm Discharge. See [text blacked out]

    Subject: non-military American civilian {photo-journalist} providing documentation of [text blacked out] and involvement in ongoing military operations. At time of action, subject observed on video [text blacked out] confiscated from [text blacked out] camera operator, also civilian, non-military, under employ of [text blacked out] and engaged under non-affiliated documentation of subject [text blacked out].

Video footage aired on satellite news feed with [text blacked out] and in news excerpt broadcasts within a twenty-four hour period ([text blacked out] 18 August, 1982). At request of Subject's family, recycles of footage were stopped by [text blacked out] and its agents, after threats of legal action by same [text blacked out]. Subsequent actions on behalf of Central Intelligence included internal investigation and memoranda supporting the closure of case file. (Items 37.9 sec. C, and, inclusive, sec. E.)

Subject reported to be in proximity of counterinsurgency [text blacked out] of which delayed by several days pending critical [text blacked out] reconnaissance and intervention. However subject witnessed in regular and protracted contact with [text blacked out] and individuals deemed "subversive" by the Guatemalan government. Subject having purported fluency or sufficient knowledge of local dialect, subject also known to associate with [text blacked out] counter to local commission curfews as instigated by Guatemalan military and jurisdictional authorities. Such claims cannot be corroborated and/or are deemed beyond the scope of this report.

Aforementioned video footage evidence indicated the perpetrator to be a youth of [text blacked out] indigenous Guatemalan nationality, age indeterminate. Weapon: modified Automatic Kalashnikov (AK-47) with 9 millimeter caliber ammunition. Weapon is typical of guerilla ("civilian") groups. Youth suspected to be agent of one Guerrilla Army of the Poor (EGP) and/or Local Irregular Forces (FIL), whose encampments at [text blacked out]. Such groups are funded in part by [text blacked out]. Investigation lies outside of the auspices of current report and neither EGP nor FIL claimed credit or knowledge of action.

[See doc. 12.6 file, classified]

Firearm discharge range of thirty yards. Ballistic and autopsy determination to be verified [remaining paragraph of text blacked out].

Expert testimony corroborates high likelihood that subject was unaware of the danger presented to his person by youth (perpetrator). [Text blacked out] subject appears to speak with perpetrator prior to arms discharge. Sound footage of poor quality determined inconclusive.

Subject survived for an indeterminate amount of time after trauma, however, [text blacked out] and lack of proper medical facilities, expertise and or action have been deemed sufficient if not conclusive for rapid acceleration of decease. Subject transported by [text blacked out] under the auspices of [text blacked out].

Firearm discharge by perpetrator determined accidental [text blacked out].

Harry sits in the kitchen of the former Mrs. Parker Thomas, amid breakfast disarray, overcooked coffee, and stale morning air.

He drove most of that Saturday morning from Los Angeles to get to Aptos, and dreaded reintroducing himself. Standing at the door of her home, holding the letter crumpled in his left fist while he pressed the hot doorbell button was to recall what it was to be a child, to want to disappear.

Of the mothers from his youth, Mrs. Thomas was all the irreducible qualities in the word woman that would remain with him indelibly. She had informed his first ideas of women, when a halo of shimmering light seemed to surround her form. That her manner spoke volumes to his pre-adolescent fantasies, this he senses she knows.

One afternoon when he was twelve she had spirited him away in her car to pick up the family dinner at the local Ponderosa steak house. Harry's mother went ballistic when he returned home too late for his own dinner. The babysitter was supposed to be looking after you! To

Harry, Mrs. Thomas had rescued him from boredom. How important he felt when they drove past his house and in fact he saw Basher sitting on the porch waiting for him.

The screenplay on Basher's life would come to light soon enough. He might yet barter with *Crown Thy Good*. To Mrs. Parker Thomas slash Dolores Burden, Harry's project might be a re-opening of a wound of the past, nothing less than Harry co-opting Basher, riding on the several years-old success of his first documentary.

He came for her blessing—and the box. But he came for her blessing primarily, good lapsed Catholic that he was.

Twenty-five years earlier Mrs. Thomas had made dramatic phone calls to him. He listened to her breakdown while trying to make sense of his friend's death, unable to get off the phone, politely waiting for her to finish, her huffing sobs, implicating. You should have been there for him, she had said, just short of laying blame on him for Nathan's wanderings into Guatemala.

She became fixated on a personal relief effort for orphaned children in Guatemala, casualties of the civil war. She had apparently corresponded with notable political figures including Rigoberta Menchú, trying to discern her group from dozens of others in that era of the Sandinistas and Iran-Contra. Asking everyone for a donation in her son's name. Harry kept his distance, uncertain about her organization, Central America Youth Relief. He thought her efforts, however well intended, misguided. He was reluctant to support any organization possibly complicit in Basher's death.

For years she sent him letters regularly. He never wrote back. He meant to.

When Harry moved to California in the early nineties, Mrs. Thomas sent him a letter. She had received a box of Nathan's personal effects that she insisted he should have. She didn't know what to do with it. It cluttered the shelf of a closet, collecting dust. Lately, she had turned a corner. She was ready to dump it in the incinerator. Knowing he lived practically next door, this might be an opportunity to visit. Reminisce. A pleasant drive. One doesn't trust the mail these days. Please just come and take it away.

Harry glanced at the letter, dismissive. He didn't want to be the guardian of Basher's high school yearbooks. He'd read the end page signatures and well wishes of all the girls he'd lusted after but to whom he hadn't existed. Basher had been practically his only friend in high school. He'd just as soon forget.

Harry tossed the letter without a second thought. For months, years, not a word from Mrs. Parker Thomas. He eventually learned of her new marriage from his father who more or less admitted an affair with Mrs. Parker Thomas when he had fallen for her at the Dry Cleaning Convention in Fresno. He imagined them getting it on and blushed at the thought, repelled by the image of his father's bald pate doing a bob over Mrs. Parker Thomas.

His mother was dying and his father was cavorting with his best friend's mother.

It almost broke up his parents.

Then, a month ago a manila envelope arrived from Dolores Burden (former Mrs. Parker Thomas), postmarked Aptos, which Harry opened while he watched the endless loop of the Rasmussen footage. In that letter the State Department report was folded primly into a hand written letter.

"You wouldn't happen to have any pictures I could borrow, would you—" Harry asks, "of Nathan?"

"Come look," she says.

He had almost forgotten visiting her in Michigan in the autumn of 1982 a few months after Basher's death when walking through her house was to be cast into the oceanic waves of her grief. He'd spent some time there before when he and Basher were kids hanging out. Harry saw then how his friend's bedroom had been turned into an airless shrine to Basher's short life and shorter career.

She leads Harry to a wall of Basher. Basher as a child, Basher at work in Lebanon, The Falkland Islands, Burkina Faso, Panama and Guatemala. Basher posing with long forgotten world dignitaries.

Daily Mrs. Thomas faced this tableau arranged for a visitor's edification. She must have taken solace in them.

Harry points to a picture of a child bundled immobile into winter wool, before Harry met him, the twilight of Nathan's innocence, before he became Basher. "Is that him?"

Mrs. Parker Thomas manages a smile that indicates her peace in the post-Nathan.

Harry scans to pictures of the two of them. Basher with Harry pulling the aluminum boat from the barn at Harry's house. One of them in the yard near Harry's family's cabin, beyond the empty space where the Kensington house ruins lay smoking.

"May I—?" he asks, reaching.

"By all means."

He lifts the photo off the wall to get a closer look. A picture from Basher's one and only semester at Michigan, standing with Harry outside of the journalism building in twenty below wind chill.

There are no photos of Parker Thomas, Basher's father. Basher had never been close to him. After Parker Thomas left them, his mother contrived a life for her son that was, by any account, pure survival. Still, Basher rebelled and ran away as soon as he could.

Harry is again distracted: an elegant woman with a red beehive suggestively wielding a vacuum hose. The glorious Ketcham Kleen Kween, Mrs. Parker Thomas, circa 1973, in a faded color advertisement for Ketcham Dry Cleaning Solvents.

Harry is almost the same age now as his father had been in '73.

"Come into the kitchen," she says, waving a coffee cup. "Tell me what's on your mind."

"Have you spoken to my father?"

"Not recently," she says.

She moves in for his cup. "Let me get you another," she says.

"That's quite all right, Mrs. Thomas."

"Mrs. Burden, really. Dolores, Harry, please. You know I've been divorced from Nathan's father for a long time. He's passed on." She nods this off with a smile and places her hand on his arm.

"As you were saying?"

He wants to ask about that village where Basher died.

Mrs. Parker Thomas had arranged a memorial ceremony all those years ago in that village somewhere in Guatemala. Harry should have attended. He agonized with guilt about staying away. Finding out later—with much relief—that the location was difficult to access. Harry's excuse was that it was too far away.

"Have you ever gone back?"

"No," she says. "It wasn't safe. The times have changed. But everyone from there that I know of is gone."

Harry gets up to carry his cup to the sink but she blocks him, moves in close. "I'm guessing you have unfinished business with Nathan," she says, gently pushing him back down in his seat. "Go ahead, darling."

Darling rings in his ears. He had couched *Deconstructing Nathan Thomas* to the studio people in elevating tones. He places his palms on the sticky table. A mistake. Maple syrup.

"I've always wondered," Harry says, "what did you do after the relief work ended?"

"It didn't stop. I set up the foundation," she says. "They're much more efficient with the needs of the community."

He slips his thumb into a pooled crescent of coffee.

"I should be getting out of your way here today, Mrs.—"

"I saw *Crown the Good*," she says.

"I'm sorry, it's 'Crown *Thy* Good.'"

"You know, Harry, I've always felt that you two were like brothers," she says. "I always suspected you might make a film about Nathan."

She couldn't know what he is planning with *Deconstructing Nathan Thomas*. That he's practically ill from having watched the videotape so much by then, the shots, his friend falling like a sack, the camera cracking beside him in the dirt, the blood, the shots, his friend, the blood.

Harry vows to give away any money he makes from the venture, to charity—rather than appearing to profit from his friend's death. By that time the shape of his ambivalent documentary would be so obvious he'd have no choice. There could be awards.

"Before I forget," she says, holding up a hand. "The reason you're here."

Mrs. Parker Thomas pulls from the counter a banker's box that is so large and heavy it slips from her hands and lands with a thud on the kitchen table, sending the remainder of his coffee sloshing, rattling the cup.

Back in Los Angeles, Harry opens the box of archives and lifts out two smaller boxes. One flat box sent from the Paris bureau of the *Agence International France Presse* still hermetically sealed in brown wrapping paper from the day they cleaned out Basher's office. The other, a Red Wing shoe box that upon breaking the seal releases an essence of mothballs and woodsmoke.

Inside the archive box are negatives and annotated proof sheets. Strictly work related.

Inside the shoe box, a chaotic bundle of 4 x 6 snapshots and half a dozen cassette tapes. Photocopied letters and unsealed envelopes and yellowed newspaper articles.

An archeology of memories.

Inundated with this trove, Harry's eye falls upon the letters lying conspicuously in the box. The one on top is addressed to him.

**Letter written in ink on torn out journal pages, postmarked Casco Viejo, Panama City, Panama. July, 1982**

I was ambivalent about writing this letter but finally, here I am doing it. That's a rough way to start but here goes anyway. I'm thinking of last time we talked and how I couldn't voice my irritation with you getting mixed up with the Paris gang, knowing they were—how to put this? Out of your league. There was jealousy on my part, I'll admit, as I still had designs on Christiane. But that was just my ego acting out—I think you could see that in Baja she was getting way more into you than she ever was into me and so I just decided to have a little fun at your expense. I know I later took it out on you when you came to Paris and I think my bluntness with you—well, I just see it was wrong, now. There was a certain amount of calculation on my part in bringing Christiane to Baja. I'm not trying to take credit for your affair. But of course I thought, I know your taste, as I know my own, who is to say that this wasn't just wild hormones acting out? I knew Bob wouldn't go for her, and if he did, how interesting that would have been anyway. It's like I actually wanted to shake her off, this is the only way I can put it. And it was before I knew her problem was as big as it was. I never thought you were ready for a woman like her, never thought you would be interested, even, but I underestimated the level of your susceptibility. When I saw you there I'd realized how seriously deep into her you were. I was bothered then because I couldn't be sure Christiane wasn't at this point stringing you along. I've come to see that wasn't the case, your actions finally convinced me. Now, I know how this must sound manipulative, to say the least. But I think that's giving me too much credit. If you think I have any interest in playing matchmaker, you overestimate my humanity. So there's your explanation. Whatever happens between you two, I give up. That woman needs a decent guy to straighten her out, but we both know we are the least viable candidates for that little career. So, what I think is, you two together? Well, go for it. You are on your own. Nothing Bash can say will really matter. I mean Harry, you have a way. Your life is so simple compared to anyone else I can think of. You keep your nose clean. I admire that. Your relationship with your family seems reasonably normal. I don't know how you see it. Maybe after the sting of my frankness wears off, you could write me back and tell me what you really think about where we stand. I could use some enlightening—I'm going to be in transit for awhile—send a letter care of the bureau, it'll get to me.

  I'm in Panama right now to deal with some family matters. My father's lived down here for awhile—I'll spare you the details. But as I was sitting here on the balcony with the sun tearing through the trees almost to the point of being unbearable, I've had some time to reflect. There's an odd bowl of the moon like a sickle, low in the sky. If I were a poet like Lorca I might make something of it. I haven't done that enough lately, haven't taken the time to write letters or keep a journal, but with my dad sick and all, I have been thinking and wondering about where I am, what I've made of my life and work.

As the agency sends me anywhere on less than twenty-four hours notice—I was lucky to use my father for an emergency break. I don't know if Rand accepted my excuse, but here I am on my father's balcony drinking an espresso from the café downstairs. It's like I'm free for the first time in four years. Now I can tell you—I don't want to go back.

Just two weeks ago, I was on the outskirts of Mombasa trying to get a ride to the airstrip. I wasn't even supposed to be working at the time because I was sick as a dog. I didn't have a translator with me. For whatever reason I think I'd been forgotten (an increasing tendency with this fucking agency), and this group of boys, three of them—kids I tell you—were approaching me. They had a gun. I did what I could to be cool and bullshitted some magic trick and when they didn't buy it I unspooled some film rolls to preoccupy them, but I was in no mood. I felt like I was being set up for something and I had no one to back me up. You think, oh, these are just kids, but it's different when you're out there awash in T.D. I don't know what I had, truthfully, but you catch my drift. I managed to walk away but who knows what could have gone down. To top it off, now I'm expected to be in a documentary that this guy Simon Rasmussen wants to do. This is out of my hands. Rand decided it was good for the agency, so Rasmussen's going to meet me in Argentina. I have no idea what he intends to film, I just know his crew is to follow me to the Falklands. I told them that absolutely I wasn't going back to the Middle East, which is where I first met him. I know he really wants to go there for his documentary, where the potential for danger is epic.

Maybe he wants to get my reaction to watching a mother standing in the freshly dug grave of her son, waving her arms as if to ward off the burial (check, saw that). Or maybe they want to see what it's like to be on a deserted street where you thought you were the only soul, only to notice three kids watching you, the biggest kid with a rifle, and you think to yourself, what does a kid playing with an automatic rifle on an empty street mean?

Initially, I was okay with Rasmussen's project. Now, having him follow me around with a camera makes me nervous, because it's this added layer of pretence about the work that compromises my protective anonymity. I'm not sure how I'm supposed to look normal on the other side of a camera. In any case, what with the recent awards and all, I have probably single-handedly given the agency the profile they want. I feel like I'm the agency's puppet sometimes, to be honest. Rand and those other guys have safe and relatively cushy office jobs. Not that I'd ever want that, however.

At first it was a kind of adrenaline rush to be on the front lines, I thought I was indestructible. But a lot has changed for me lately. I've met a woman that I'm going to see when I go to Buenos Aires. I expect she'll come with me and I can retire temporarily or at least take three months off and not even look at Rand's itinerary. I'm not saying more right now because I always get ahead of myself when it comes to the L-word and things are very unpredictable right now. It's not perfect, it never is, but she's a big reason I wanted to stop the train wreck for awhile. She's from a completely different culture—just like charming Christiane, and I guess my being from Michigan, that's really appealing. I'll admit, she's young, too. It isn't always easy. I know her family probably expects her to stay in Mexico City and help out with the family business—but I can make her life exciting, I think. They left Argentina two years ago and she's the only one who was bold enough to return. She's been my inside information source during the war. Next I'm going down to the Falklands to take some pictures at this collectivist farm—very low key, you might say, except that it's in the Falklands.

Her English is not so great and maybe that's how we connected, physically, you know. I have a buzzing in my gut and stomach waiting to see her again. I don't know where it stands, to be honest, and so all of my energy is spent trying to figure that out. She's almost the opposite of me—very quiet, frankly doesn't smile very much, a little skittish, but she just gets under my skin like no woman ever has. To see her you might think she's tormented. At first I thought she was, but when I see her smile breaking through, if just to be polite—it is such a natural smile. She lifts me up, somehow, even after all the tempests that we go through. She is passionate.

Coming to Panama has been a reunion of sorts for my father and me. I can't say that it's all been gravy, but when you are staring at the source huffing to take a breath and the first comment out of his mouth is to ask why you're there, or to exclaim how it is a miracle you're (I am) still alive—to be genuinely shocked, yet indifferent—is to know your place in his world. This man who hurt my mother so casually years ago—he doesn't exist for her anymore. I realized that I have to take the high road. Like, if complaining to me that my existence doesn't matter makes him feel better, what should I care? I don't. I'm here out of conscience. Let's just put it this way, the obvious has long been lost on Colonel Parker Thomas.

My mother understands when I tell her I thought I should be here. I think she'll be glad when he finally goes away. I almost wasn't going to tell her I was here but we talked on the phone last night. She would have found out or maybe knew, I think, like there's a psychic connection mothers have to sons. I didn't stay on the phone long enough to go into details.

I worry about my mother because I know if she hears where I'm going second hand she goes a bit nuts. This can be like a betrayal to her.

I really am coming to a point where I'd be ready to quit this work. It's like I've proven myself to everyone that I needed to prove myself to, (mainly myself) and I wonder, why not settle down now, have a family and all that? Go set up and live in Central America somewhere where there's an unmolested beach. I've been thinking about investing in real estate. A simpler life is what I crave. When I see how most of the world lives, and yet how welcoming they are to me in these strange corners, I see the writing on the wall. I've already made enough money to live on for a year or so, and what says I have to buy into the ragged American dream? It took me a long time to decide, but I don't think I'll be coming back stateside to stay. I'll visit my mother of course, but I've been away enough to know that life is far more interesting for me the further I go.

I'm glad to be idle here. Strangers attempt to talk to me and I feel perfectly content to revel in my gringo roots. I could feel this way anywhere, probably, but this is why I've more or less decided that if I settle down, it will be in Central America somewhere. I used to imagine I needed to learn every language of every country I stepped foot in, and yet the one it would most benefit me to learn, Spanish, is probably the one I know the least of.

Then again, I'm not sure if I'm cut out for domesticity. I know I am my father's son, as much as I am fighting it, by my itinerant life. He had me and was gone before he could even get to know much of our life in that town. On the other hand, I'm not convinced my mother was loyal from the get go. I don't know if she had a choice with a husband like that. Guess it runs in the family.

I've avoided getting caught up in the traditional trappings, the attempt to get what your neighbor has, as if the getting will make you happy. Envy is the worst vice. We have always been opposed in that way. I say that as much because I imagine you stopped reading four pages ago. How could I be envious of you, you might ask? May we some day size each other up as equals.

I wouldn't recommend this work for you, after all, by the way. I know you asked me once. There's a guy I know at the agency, he looks at me as his project, oddly enough, and he's always telling me the twenties are the hardest place to be in life—but who knows, sooner or later we get old and it's just another decade.

In the cafe downstairs my dad's photographs are all over the walls. The two guys that run the place, Seluard and Jeremiah, I don't know if they're gay or they're brothers or what. They can appear to be both at once, if that seems possible. And there's this character Obregon with a Che beard who hangs out in the café. All day long, coffee after coffee, cigarette upon cigarette, he draws these surreptitious sketches of patrons who sit there. You don't notice until he drops by your table and deals your caricature to you face down on the back of a placemat. The guy knows my father pretty well going on twenty years, and he's done so many portraits of the Colonel that the owner has framed a few and hung them on the wall. There's one, it's as old as their friendship and the resemblance to yours truly is disconcerting. I have a big enough ego to have wondered how he'd done it, since I'd never been there before. When I walked in there for the first time, all the regulars even did a double take.

When Seluard found out, he started calling me "Junior Parker." I was not amused and am quite sick of it.

Panama City is nothing remarkable, but my father lives in a grand old place here that could have come out of L'enfant's Paris. I'm not here to sightsee, and have spent plenty of time in duller places. If you squint your eyes as you look North, you can imagine your are living on the Left Bank at the turn of the century, but for the sirens, the cars, and the fish stink coming from the bridge. I guess you get this in any old city, but this part of town was built by the French. I can almost pretend I'm right at home—Paris, that is, if I could even say that's home. And if I stay too long, I'm afraid they're going to offer me my father's job at *La Prensa*.

Far be it for me to be critical of my father's work, but basically, he's a snuff photographer. I'm thinking of Weegee's style perhaps, or like in L.A. around the time of prohibition, the guys who shot car wrecks in all their mangled glory, or the gangland murders in flea bag hotels. There's a lot of gang crime here, and if he doesn't get to the scene, he just shows up at the morgue and takes a picture of the body for page one. He never runs out of bodies. Clearly, we work on a different scale.

I've of course been snooping around here, much as I know I shouldn't. He's my father, what could he possibly have to hide from me now? You may be disappointed to learn that little was found to incriminate the Colonel in any sort of subversive activities. I suspect his housekeeper, who doesn't do actual cleaning, was probably set loose on the premises before I arrived with a set of keys to lock away the evidence from my prying eyes.

The place reeks. I never realized how much my father smokes, but it permeates everything here. Even the inside of his refrigerator has a coating of nicotine. I took it upon myself to clean the place top to bottom. In the mornings I get up early, take one of Seluard's coffees out onto the balcony, and write letters. The world ignores me while I'm here. I'm almost unknown. It feels good to let myself go AWOL.

Perhaps I've come to peace with him, I don't really know if it matters. He is in and out of consciousness after a complicated heart operation, which was bad to begin with because of his history of health issues, then there was an infection of some sort, and they say it's a matter of weeks, perhaps days. I will sound crass to admit this, but I'm not sure he will be missed—at least not by his own family. I am here out of obligation and yet I can tell you I want to feel something, generosity perhaps, but pity and unease is all that I come up with.

Twenty-three feels like a milestone to me. I've already done and accomplished more than some of the forty year olds in the agency. I sometimes feel I'm only complaining about my hardships when I've really had it easy. I've never had to look for work, I've never had to scrape for a meal, all by lucking out on this gig. But I just want a break. Something simpler. I don't know what that's like. I realize I'm not supposed to think this, but isn't it a crisis when one can't deal with their freedom? Beyond some technical knowledge I have, I'm plunked down in the middle of hell and I have to document it. Some call this survival.

I sometimes wonder if these images have been burned on my soul.

The guy I was talking about, let's just call him my mentor, he went through this when he was my age, and he wasn't anywhere near as successful as I've been. It doesn't matter, it's the same shit, just with a gold plated shovel.

I don't identify with any of the other photogs in the agency. I work alone, I don't even want to work with anyone. Most of them don't have the luxury of being set up the way I am. I think this quality is one that I hang on to in my pride. It works for me, Harry, but I don't know how well it will serve you. You must ultimately be the judge of that. I doubt sometimes that what I say will get through to you.

When I talked about Lebanon, I don't think I was truthful in my answer. What I meant to say is that as soon as I'm no longer scared, I'll know it's time to get out. But confronting my father's death is a wake up call because I have no idea how it will affect me. If I knew my parents still had some regard for each other it wouldn't seem like such a weight to carry. But of course they don't. And they didn't, perhaps from the moment I was conceived. That messes with you. I don't know what I'm supposed to feel.

In some way it's easier for me to say all this in a letter, I just get to let out this long exhale and know you will read it on your own sweet time. It makes no difference to me. I know that it matters more that I got to say my piece, probably more so than it does for you to hear it (read it). Someone told me, once.

I'm moving on, soon—like I said, to the Falklands and then up to Mexico City to meet the Miradors, and I wonder how they will take to me. I know, sounds serious.

I've got other business in Mexico. There's a fellow who put on a show of some of my photographs I took when I was in Guatemala, and he's been trying to get me to come to the Yucatan—I'm not sure that I want to keep myself in the limelight so to speak on my down time, but people start making all kinds of appeals and the agency decides for me where I go, which is one of the great drawbacks of not being a freelancer. It probably is the drawback. Even when I pretend that it has nothing to do with me, which is usually the truth, I still somehow get sucked in. I had no idea what I was in for when I signed on with an international agency, and it was impossible for me to imagine when I was running around in high school with that camera that I'd end up here. Of course, this is to sound disingenuous, as if I don't take responsibility for my work, but sometimes I feel like as long as it continues beyond my own interest in people, in their lives—when the work objectifies them—I have no purpose. And yet that's the definition of my work. But I can't imagine what else I would want to do.

I'll leave off with a line of verse I read just this morning:

Si muero

Dejad el balcon abierto.

Harry is googly-eyed, beaded with sweat, caught up in the mesmeric loop of the videotape of Basher's last breath when Janelle calls down from the top of the stairs. Something in her tone worries. Scribbling notes in a legal pad, he knows he can't keep the evidence hidden for long. In his windowless workspace in the basement of her house, she asks him what he is wrecking his eyes over. He replies with a timid, "Um, editing."

    He'd freighted significance onto this film in an attempt to pitch it to the studio heads. He'd set up the video and replayed it for himself continuously, imagining a narrative line, ancillary characters, some composites. Of a story he had threads. Maybe it could involve drug and gun runners, although this probably wasn't far off the mark.

    As soon as Janelle had seen the Rasmussen footage Harry had begun packing to go south, first the Yucatan, then Central America. Post-arthroscopic knee surgery. It didn't seem fair to insist that it was only research. How many times could he watch his friend die?

    Harry was soon off to Mexico for the meeting with one of the people Basher's father had been close to, then on to Guatemala. Aided and abetted by Harry's agent, Greenglass, whom, when he had given him the go ahead, probably expected the five grand up front as an advance on a first draft of the screenplay; the money would facilitate a round up of talking heads interviews like those that had been praised in *Crown Thy Good*. These could later be filmed and edited into the as yet amoebic, *Deconstructing Nathan Thomas*.

He keeps the banker's box hidden, and is circumspect with Janelle on why he watches the film of this once renowned photojournalist taking a Sisyphean fall. He can only downplay it for so long.

Janelle seems to understand.

"Maybe a week away could be good for you. Harry?"

The Rasmussen footage is part of a mosaic. For all of the action it contains, it reveals less about his friend than the photograph stacks before him. Or the letters. It contains the end game, the symbolic resolution that he hopes informs the life that might otherwise be forgotten. It is a replay, the fast forward and slow-mo, the part about Basher's life he needed to conjure to get to the real Nathan. That letter, it feels like it could have been written last week.

## Radio Interview Transcript. March, 1982

BBC

    We're speaking today with Mr. Nathan Thomas, a photojournalist for the French International Press Agency who is courting some controversy in his methods, to say the least, as revealed this week to an unwitting reporter at the *Times*. Is that how you would characterize it, Mr. Thomas?

THOMAS

    Characterize what?

BBC

    You will admit that the *Times* reporter remarked upon and took you to task on your unorthodox style—

THOMAS

>Right.

BBC

>—in which you don't look at what you are photographing. Can you talk about that?

THOMAS

>Well, I use a lot of film. This way I know that I'll get the action. Even if I don't know half the time what it will be.

BBC

>Now let me ask you then—how do you know what's in the viewfinder?

THOMAS

>You don't, really. Just indirectly. It's the style of camera I use. It's the way I walk around what I'm trying to take pictures of.

BBC

>How did this start for you—this method?

THOMAS

>Most of the papers want evidence of someone being there. I'm in this way like a monkey with a camera. I can just wander around and sooner or later I'm going to get an important document. It's also safer for me, because then I can get tricky shots where no one is on to me.

BBC

That's a rather shocking pronouncement. So you don't ever see your subject?

THOMAS

Okay, I'll grant you, once in awhile I have to pay attention to a subject. But as soon as I do, I stop.

BBC

You stop looking.

THOMAS

No. I stop taking pictures.

BBC

Really?

THOMAS

Yes. But there are other times. I don't always *not* look. On some days I'm like a giant set of eyes. On those days I don't take as many photos. Once you start looking too much, you stop seeing.

BBC

So tell me, do you or do you not take pictures without looking?

THOMAS

I definitely do. Sometimes I don't. It's a long story ... Where do I begin? You take a lot of pictures. A lot. That makes up for not looking in a couple of ways. First of all, because when you take hundreds of pictures, sooner or later you'll get one that works, that has every quality you need in it. In fact, this one usually jumps out at me when I'm in the darkroom . . . Also, I think the more time you spend taking the pictures overrides the fact that you aren't looking, because you spend twice as much time taking pictures and so sooner or later you are thought to be like every other journalist out there with a camera. It's like, hey, this guy must be a photographer.

BBC

    Are you teasing out a metaphor?

THOMAS

    I guess I would say, examine the work and decide for yourself.

BBC

    What is the purpose of doing it this way?

THOMAS

    There is no point, other than it works for me.

BBC

    Do your colleagues know you do this?

THOMAS

    Well, it's not like I keep it a secret.

BBC

The photographs are the evidence, you'd say.

THOMAS

Yes. The agency always gets their shot.

BBC

Would you consider yourself versed in the art of photography?

THOMAS

Not particularly. I mean, it's not art.

BBC

No?

THOMAS

Listen. I think because I started out with the opposing notion, that in fact it wasn't an art form—I tend to get people who insist on arguing this. But I'm pretty clear about what I do.

BBC

Yet there is a long tradition in the art of photography.

THOMAS

I understand that. But it's a different approach for me. I do my work my way, I've trained myself so that I know what I want to capture. A specific shot. I mean you become so adept that you pretty much know where to go to get the picture that you want. And along with that you sometimes have to meet a certain individual's expectations. Your editors, your boss. You know what to take, you know where to go. It's an implicit understanding. No one sends me in there and says, get a picture of Idi Amin. But, you know when you get to Uganda, you're damn well going to get a picture of him.

BBC

    What led you into this work?

THOMAS

    It gave me a lot of freedom. Freedom to travel. To go to interesting places.

BBC

    Do you have some political motivation?

THOMAS

    You mean like running for office or something?

BBC

    No. In terms of your subject matter.

THOMAS

    No. None.

BBC

    The decision wasn't as spontaneous as your solipsistic approach?

THOMAS

No, no. Of course not. I mean, I did win a few awards and some recognition, but getting to do this work is as much about my desire to travel, truth be told.

BBC

You are very young. Do you ever think you'll tire of the photographer's life?

THOMAS

Ask me next year.

BBC

What has been the most difficult task in the work you do?

THOMAS

The most difficult part is facing the unpleasantness. And smelling it, too. Literally. I won't go into it. It can be pretty overwhelming. But you're there with a job to do. You realize that you chose this job because in some way you feel a calling. That compulsion is drawing you there. Someone is asking you to help.

BBC

How do you cope with the danger that you must confront day after day?

THOMAS

Sometimes the danger is not so obvious. It's more of a sense that you can get. Context of the situation. Being in a country that's in the middle of a civil war is particularly harrowing. Because, you often . . . the rules change.

BBC

    Could you elaborate on this a bit more?

THOMAS

    In some ways, there are no rules. And, I try to make contact with people. I try to look them in the eyes and . . . get a sense of their humanity. This is necessary when I feel like I'm in danger.

BBC

    Can you give us an example?

THOMAS

    When someone considers us members of the press corps as their enemy, for instance.

BBC

    So you have—you've had to face someone in that situation—you are their enemy?

THOMAS

    It's inevitable. They can turn on you, at some point. I suppose the rationalization I make to myself is that I'm a neutral voice, neutral eyes, there. I'm there to give witness. Everyone wants a witness. Every one. I don't care who you are . . . you believe in your cause. And . . . that's why you're fighting.

BBC

What do you say to someone who says, "Anyone can do this work, just give me the camera and I'll go there and take the picture?"

THOMAS

Well, first of all, that's extremely naïve. Most people would not choose to go there. You know, as a member of the press bureau, I am allowed certain access. There's a kind of glorification—the romantic side—of the job that I do, but, on the day to day of it, it is just a job just like any other. Perhaps the difference is that I travel endlessly. My life is put in danger with some frequency. And . . . I tend to just . . . I tend to have to deal with situations that the average person will never want to deal with. As romantic as it may seem, you have to want it. I suppose I want it.

BBC

So by this fact, there is some talent in what you do—that must indicate that you have an aptitude.

THOMAS

I suppose.

BBC

Contrary to what you have said about it not being art.

THOMAS

Well, art, if you think about it, is artifice. I'm not denying artifice. So, perhaps I'm not denying art after all.

BBC

So, what do you call yourself, if you are not an artist?

THOMAS

I'm a documentarist.

BBC

A documentarist?

THOMAS

Exactly. Just what it sounds like. I document.

BBC

A very un-disciplined type of documenting, wouldn't you say?

THOMAS

I would not.

BBC

Just the way that you work, it seems almost haphazard.

THOMAS

It is haphazard. It's just that it became, I don't know, more interesting for me to do it this way . . . Look, it's about how do you cope out there taking photos of people dying? I'm ambivalent about that. Believe me.

Off the record? I'm actually advised not to talk about this.

BBC

Maybe that's why you don't look.

THOMAS

Perhaps.

BBC

This brings up a topic I'm interested to hear about. How do you explain the retrospective—"Nathan Thomas Against the Grain," at the Sylvian—with that trenchant write up on the images from, where was it, Guatemala?

THOMAS

Yes.

BBC

How do you explain a retrospective at your age?

THOMAS

Someone asked me—an associate of my father's—to put some of my pictures together for a show. I thought, why not? It's not like I felt that I was going to have to put words alongside the pictures. The images speak for themselves. That's not my writing about the pictures, by the way. The end result fits my argument. If you'll notice, none of the pictures in that show have any semblance to art. That's just my opinion.

BBC

    That's not the opinion of the *Times* critic.

THOMAS

    What can I say? I'm telling you, I'm like the millionth monkey.

BBC

    I'll take your word for it, Nathan Thomas. But I don't see it, and I doubt a lot of folks who you've touched with your work will feel that way.

THOMAS

    So be it.

# II. MEMORY

Human beings are drawn to the idea that death holds some profound, metaphysical meaning.

When it happened, Harry wanted to believe that the child who had a gun, the military presence, the time and place and slant of light, all had a meaning. And it does in retrospect, in revision, because of the pointless moment culminating his friend's twenty-three years, meted out on a gravel two track alongside a grange, tucked between jungle and river, under blue skies and birds of a million colors and calls.

Basher's letters were balms in his absence, read and re-read for hidden clues. He had told him, "Come to Guatemala, man. You can have an entire beach to yourself." It was an unfamiliar land on whose shores Basher had surfed, because he could, because no one else did. Yet, as in every place in the world he went to, when he had been there he had made it familiar and demystified, even in the shadow of military activity and government corruption, as he'd said in another letter, unconvincingly. And the constant revision he'd make about how he could go into the *world, on his terms, to a place where the disenfranchised don't think twice about showing a* gringo rubia *with an expensive camera where he should go.*

The shots: someone whacking the broad side of a two by four on the plywood enclosure above their heads.

The ring in his ears, a struck tuning fork. Unbearably loud and, catching the recoil in his aiming hands, painful. All in the name of research. What he notices is the tang of cordite, the listless smoke curtained between plywood barriers. At the shot the butt is jolted into his left hand, as if catching it in a slammed door. The sudden numb sting is so abrupt he doesn't immediately notice it. When he looks at his hand, two divots are seeping blood. Battle scars, he'll think to tell Janelle later. When the shots ping, each squeeze and snap of the trigger feels delayed. Just as he pulls it to click he thinks the shot will go, but he grips tighter, no shot comes out. This is the Derringer. Tricky little bastard. Loud, too. That's a shot gun shell. When the shot snaps off, it's all he can do to control his aim, which is high and wide. The instantaneous thump of the plywood with the pop of the gun is disorienting, distracting. He feels always a half second out of synch with it. His hands feel raw, stunned and numb from the shooting. Where he looks on his hands, the points of contact have been pinched and abraded. And the tinnitus of a high toned electronic whistle drills through his head, in spite of earplugs.

Harry considers the equation of the shooter down the gates. He doesn't feel he's worthy of title, a name. He's the likes you'd cross the road to avoid. This one has entertained career crime. He gathers this from a predilection for mind numbing reality television about cops, where the police in Dade or Hillsborough County corral the day's offenders. This guy wouldn't think too much about using the gun. Either that or he's trying to impress his girlfriend as he stands in front of her with the gun, a Glock, standard cop piece. She's all of eighteen, oddly seasoned and unfazed by the insistent assault of automatic fire at the target, unaffected by the fog of gunpowder.

**January, 1978**

The picture of Basher isn't even at Harry's Grandmother's—but he thinks of it anyway. Taken up there, in Michigan. Harry had gone back so many times for family matters that his Gram was always an object of those trips.

On flights back to Detroit Metro Harry would be seated next to little talkative ladies whom he'd gamely endure from California that reminded him of his Gram. They would invite him over for lunch or a game of cards as if he lived next door, suggesting that he meet this or that grandniece of theirs, until Harry had to tell them his real age (he was always mistaken for ten years younger). He couldn't help but wonder about their need to see in him a surrogate grandson they might appreciate; he took the invitations graciously and said that he would be pleased to stop in next time he was in Lexington (never). One woman was a ringer for Gram Ogletree, except that he was certain the woman was in fact at least two decades younger than her.

Gram Ogletree stood firm and resolute like the mast of a ship, the last thing to disappear out on the horizon. She clearly wasn't dying the way we all are, he thought. She was going to sail into old age and quit on her own terms. He'd fairly thought she might outlive them all. Like Lady Sak K'uk of the Maya, who had ruled her roost. She had reigned over everyone and had become immortal. That was Gram Ogletree. Gram made the bluehairs he met on the plane seem insubstantial. She was beginning to show sparks of battyness, perhaps only simple misunderstandings, mishearings. Occasionally, Harry saw what he thought was a moment of worry in his Grandmother's face, an almost imperceptible suggestion in her eyes that she didn't think all was smooth sailing. He didn't want to believe it, he didn't ever ask. It was his trade-off. His grandmother thought his projects all very considerable and worthwhile. She gave him money if he needed. She was an indispensable ally.

With Basher, Harry was listening to NPR on the radio driving in Northern Michigan, trying to get to his grandmother's house near the Potawatomi Indian reservation. Winter cold, winterlong, the air freezing in the nostrils and pinching them shut while the sunlight warms and crackles the ice rimed passage. Northern Michigan was tough; Harry wasn't tough enough for it anymore. Besides, he'd only ever had visits there, thankful he'd had the chance to visit; glad he didn't grow up there.

The landscape at Gram's always made him think of death for some reason. It was basically a ghost town. The cold north abandoned, the proximity to the Indian reservations, the long, meandering, frequently potholed roads that crossed rusting rail tracks that disappeared into weedy industrial lots, the thin walled boxy houses that sat isolated on open plains with small windows shrouding threadbare curtains; in the whiff of moldering lumber piles the odor of failed commerce. Streets named after tree species of forests long sawn down to fire the smelting furnaces that sat cold. Railroad tracks veined through abandoned granges and virgin timber land from former railroad empires built and burned by silver mining at the turn of the century. There was a sense of a perpetual autumn, the monotone of resignation and unemployment overheard in the voice of the last shopkeeper in town.

Harry took him to the places of his youth, because they fascinated Basher. Basher had never brought Harry to any of his. He thought, perhaps rightly, that Basher didn't have any. There is a visit to see Harry's grandmother, in the middle of a deep freeze, Harry regaling Basher with the story of her boarder, Larry; Larry's story of tragicomic proportions, a grotesquerie, as Harry thought of it, disturbed as he was when he first learned of it and wanted to say, *Oh Grammaw!*

Catching the undeniable whiff of a tuberose bush—or was it the Pond's hand cream smell?—Harry thought of his grandmother's and saw the rosebushes at the side of her house. These dim summery memories led him indoors, to the scratchy woven acrylic throws that for years she had carefully hand knitted and stretched across the couch (it was always too cold at 45.39 degrees North Latitude.) To return to these sensory flights, he could see himself all over again, the unhappy boy in grey corduroy pants sitting through afternoon soaps, waiting for his father to pick him up.

The memories from his childhood, when he could hide his fantasy life in a shoe box. He had, in retrospect, never been a very self-aware child. He had only been able to understand why his father took him away through the retrospection of self-knowledge, years of experience and blunt reality.

As a child Harry sat here and waited for his father to relieve him of his self-enclosed world. His father was working, supposedly, although it took Harry several years to realize that his father was having an affair with Mrs. Thomas. It seemed a miracle that his father had spurned from Gram and the grandfather Harry'd never known, a big man with oversize hands and an unhealthy grimace he'd studied in the only black and white photo he'd ever seen of him. His father, possibly at the age of ten, seems to be rubbing the back of his head where presumably his father had just whacked him with those mitts, his father crouched down behind at the Michilmackinaw crossing (in the forties, before the bridge) his stinging farmer's hands hang at ease between two wide spaced knees. Where had his father gotten his gentleness from? His mother—Harry's gram? Each succeeding generation of the Ogletree men had become softer, less brutish, more self-consciously inward looking. Janelle often accused Harry of being passive—she was convinced that he was trying too hard to be accepted, that his mother must have been afraid for him and had made him a softy. Harry had never told her that his mother was dead long before he could account for any of her psychological impact on his life.

Harry sat with Basher at the Cedar Grill in Maple City.

"Now when we get to Gram's house, you're going to see a funny looking guy," Harry said, preparing his friend. "Maimed. He's had a rough life, no doubt about it."

Two Native Americans were arguing, lubricated by drink. The fisticuffs looked like it was heating up. Basher ordered two shots of Jim Beam, one for each of them, downed his in a dash. Harry sat placidly and looked at his. "I can just sip it," Harry said. "Right?"

Basher looked at Harry. "Since when have you sipped your Whisky?"

Harry had spent summers up here, occasionally skiing at Mirror lake, and he knew these regulars at the Cedar Grill were pushovers in a sense, they were always fighting for honor or something, and it rarely involved outsiders. Still, Harry expected one of the men to pull out a knife at some point, or worse, a gun.

Harry began. "So there were these two brothers who lived on this reservation, Larry and Sitka, Larry was the younger of the two. And one day they were drinking and they got the idea to get revenge on these guys that had stolen the stereo from Sitka's car. Larry wanting to impress his brother, decided to get out his grandfather's old thirty-ought-six. He'd used it to shoot cans and signs down by the railroad tracks, but hadn't really known much about the gun, didn't know it's power at close range, other than it sprayed these signs with pellets. The other part of this is that Sitka was kind of having an affair with this girl, one of the sisters of the guy who stole the stereo—or at least they thought this was the guy who stole the stereo. So Larry and Sitka decided to get into Sitka's four barrel Camaro and go down there with the gun and show them what was what. Now it was a cold day and there was ice on the porch, and Larry ran in the house to get the gun while Sitka waited in the car. As Larry came charging out with the gun, he somehow slipped and the gun hit him under his chin, firing off. And Sitka saw this from the car, and must have freaked out, and ran over to his brother, and thought he was dead. So Sitka took the gun and turned it on himself. Killed himself. Meanwhile Larry's laying there and he's pretty screwed up, his face is pretty much toast. And his brother is dead beside him. Long story short?

Eventually they took care of Larry, and he kind of got back to reasonable normalcy."

Harry kept the details in reserve, frankly not wanting to make it graphic.

"But now he's left with . . . this face."

Harry talked about the drinking, the life on the reservation, his grandmother's teaching at their school for so many years. She had known Larry since he was a boy, when he was a student of hers until he became a casualty of the tribe's fall into dereliction.

Harry never had the nerve to get to know Larry, which required talking to him, looking at him, asking—rather probing—into his life.

"You'll see," he said, with a wide eyed knowingness that managed to accentuate his unfortunate pride at having a story up on Basher. "He just sits in his rocking chair in her living room," Harry says. "He's a sweet guy, really. Gram hangs with him and feeds him pureed carrots, stuff like that. Baby food. He can communicate, he's normal in so many ways, it's just that he's strange to look at. Pug they call him, or used to. It seems cruel, but it was a joke. Pug. I call him Larry, of course."

"Of course," Basher says.

"Larry is a child, a baby. Sweet-natured like a baby. To be honest? The accident was the best thing that could have happened to him, in a sense. He never knew a woman, you know what I mean. At least, not that we know of.

"He's got a good life, in some way. He's no longer bothered by any of that stuff that usually gets you into trouble when you come from such a life. And Gram is an amazing woman. So, I'm telling you this so you don't freak out when you see him. You can look, of course, he's definitely an odd looking one, but I would say look long enough to get the sense of him, but don't stare. He's self-conscious."

Harry could see the story had made an impression on Basher.

"So you haven't gotten to know him," Basher says.

"I've just related what I know. Wanted to prepare you for a shock."

"You say it like that's what he is. A shock."

"No disrespect to Larry," Harry said. "I'm just telling you."

"Harry, you strike me as the kind of person who watches the news to be a voyeur."

"Really?" Harry says. "Come on."

Gram Ogletree had spent her life in this house, her marriage house, squat and shoe box shaped with dilapidated siding that was, however unusually, well insulated. She kept her mail in the freezer, a kind of preservation. When Harry stayed there, he was not put up in the guest room, the room where everything eventually ended up, newspapers and magazines and yarn bundles. Rotary club pamphlets. An oval black and white photograph, with a convex front, hung from the wall looking over a bed in the guest room—his great grandmother and grandfather Ogletree, in stovepipe collars, their birdlike eyes piercing otherwise expressionless faces, his great grandfather's slicked and glinting jet black hair. This was Gram's boarder Larry's room, though Larry often fell asleep in his chair in the living room.

This was Harry's family's place of origin. His father had moved them to Abel, moved them away from the rustic and sadly beautiful part of Michigan to open his failed dry cleaning business. The connection to the land and remoteness that kept one out of reach of needing much more had preserved Mrs. Ogletree. Gram had settled comfortably into her old age, and she was content. She made friends easily with all the neighbors, though the closest ones were a mile away. The Kittredge boy shoveled out her driveway for a few dollars every winter, and brought her groceries when she couldn't get around. She still drove an old Ford Town car, which was a minor miracle, and cause of concern for the family.

Harry never saw his Gram in other places than that house. Her chair was her throne. In the light coming in he was unnerved to see cobwebs on the seat backs of the dining room chairs.

Harry tactlessly pointed. "Gram, do you clean?" Harry's breath pearled in the sunlight.

"We never use them," Gram said.

Harry sees through the lace doily curtains Basher leading Larry by the arm, like two old friends in corduroy coats on the thin ice that left a film on the driveway, the same drive Harry used to shovel nearly every winter visit.

"Your friend has nice manners," Mrs. Ogletree confided to Harry. Harry had to stop himself from a readymade response because he thought this comment was to the indictment of his own lack of manners. His grandmother was prim and infinitely polite and she could occasionally surprise him with a salty phrase, but rarely an unkind one.

Basher and Harry were ten years younger than Larry, or so, and he'd wonder if maybe Larry and Basher had found in each other surrogate brothers. Larry being an older brother or even the absent father in Basher's life, and Basher being to Larry like his lost older brother, Sitka.

Harry got an earful from Basher, on the drive back, the human story filling in the blunt details of the accident. Or maybe he heard it from someone else, in memory it was Basher's version, associated with Basher befriending Larry, whom Harry had only ever had brief words with, usually about *The Rockford Files*.

Basher had been moved by the brother's act of despair and self-erasure.

"I just get this feeling," Basher said in the car, "it's an uncanny connection. He's suffered so much in his life. He told me he has a girlfriend."

"She's blind, grammaw says."

"Sure. But I guess she did that visioning thing with her hands, he said, where she touched his face. So she could see him. It's not only like that. She sees him, too, his soul. Kind of what I'm talking about."

"Right."

"I know you do that, too," Basher said.

"What?"

"See his soul."

Harry was dubious, and quite convinced he never saw anyone's soul.

"I doubt it," Harry said.

"Harry. Such a rationalist."

"No, I'm just saying. I need evidence."

"Okay, consider it a figure of speech."

"Maybe you don't see his soul, you just . . . I don't know, feel his soulfulness," Harry said.

"You got it."

"Well, I don't know if I'm capable."

"Sure you are."

"I mean, I'd need to be open to it. And I'm just put off by him, picking at those eye things and all."

"It's just his face. Nothing wrong there. Just what happened."

"Exactly."

"But he's a person, too."

"I'm not denying that."

"It's just the way you said it, Harry. The way you told me his story. He's not the thing that happened to him."

"I can't get past that thing."

"Right, besides, he told me he knows when people are looking at him funny. But get this, he's not bothered by it. He's so used to it."

"Maybe you have the right approach—but the guy has always just freaked me out a bit."

"No kidding."

So it was that Basher did what he would become so good at, burning in the light in the darkroom onto the random detail, the piece to make the other pieces fall into place. And this enlarged him, made him the perfectionist of his life, as if such knowledge was the only thing that mattered in that journey.

Harry thinks there is something larger to what Basher said, and Basher doesn't do anything to deny this effect. Basher could easily set off Harry—he was too rapt an audience. It was as if Basher was aware that he had some lesson he had to impart to the world.

"This is about relationships, Harry. And I'm not talking about with girls. You might get that with girls once in awhile—take your sister, for instance—"

"My sister?"

Basher put his arm on the door, as if getting ready to expound a theory. "But not in sexual or romantic ways. I'm talking the meeting of the minds. The other way is a lost cause for that. I'm just hoping you get this, before we go our separate ways—before you go off to college. It's the thing no one's going to tell you about. Well, I am—you know what I mean."

The long drive back through Michigan winter fields painted white and ice cold, with religious blue shadows and steam that came out of his mouth crackling in the air. And a longing, a self-knowledge rising, losing him, Basher was going to the exact opposite side of the world of painted sand colored and dry, and hot, with countries full of Larrys, Harry knew. And in these quiet moments of reflection, alone with Basher in the car, Harry wondered if he too, couldn't be one of them.

What Harry sees, heightened by the oxycodone, an endless loop.

The popping of bullets swaying through the equatorial haze laying Basher out like Quetzacoatl's alms. (That's Aztec, wrong.) Just before he falls, a cartoon coyote, he notices his new ventilated torso, only in this world he doesn't get an orchestration for his plop. He's not falling from a rocky ledge with an anvil roped around his waist or riding a crate of dynamite into a chasm courtesy ACME & Company, falling onto a painted desert, motion lines like black rubber bands snapping after him in a celluloid utopia, only to be revived after the fifth fall and to be deaccessioned yet again to the material world by Chuck Jones and Fritz Freling for one more impossible dispatch. Instead, he falls, Basher, improbably first rate photojournalist, face forward, onto his Hasselblad with a soft suck, full stop, mouth full of dirt, breaking teeth, while five bullets riddle the chest. Got it all. Action, tragedy, comedy.

He writes a bit of dialogue, (the words spoken between Basher and the boy with the gun, to his knowledge, went unrecorded) to access the tale, to sympathize with the other side:

*You, white man!*

(The boy speaks in Spanish, of course.)

*I'm big daddy with gun.*

Perhaps this fillip makes it too oddly premeditated. He could work in the references that the Mayans sacrificed the young of their quarry in flaming skyward rituals. Harry (who's he kidding?), has had years of Hollywood reversals and attendant misgivings—why dramatize? As in, if the place exists and there's no one there to experience it, how will they know that it isn't all created on a soundstage in Culver City, anyway? Yet it's such a good story, it'll put him back on the map. He waits, thinks, remembers and ruminates, all set to write, investigate, rather, to elucidate, after a fifth drunken toast at Loo Wei Oak from which every re becomes a de, becoming the deconstructing of Basher Thomas. The homage becomes the bounty, the world fills him and leaves him longing for clarity. The wolf is not at the door, the wolf fills the void. When all is sound and color, he strains to do one simple thing, when he could imagine his friend's life not clouded by a gross commercial display.

That half minute videotape says all that is entertaining of the death of the life, but yea, though obsessed as it has rendered him, the knowledge, the heat of this being, the ineffable qualities, if only these were possible to ... For you have touched this person, and your memories die with you. You can find all who may have known him on this troubled earth, and touched him, all the collisions of diverse personalities. Artifacts and memories fading, cut to fade, a single grainy distant shot with one minute of artificial sound.

It's been twenty-five years. The child who pulled the trigger he imagines may never have had a childhood. Is now a man, if he's still there, if he has not been deaccessioned in the material world himself, the signifier becoming the signified. But then Harry doesn't need to stress that for his agent.

**November, 1980**

Arms draped on shoulders. Basher has become a different person after his brief yet remarkable taste of the world since moving to Paris and joining the French Agency. His power over Harry remains, has grown stronger.

Harry rarely sees him. There is one semester Basher floats around the Michigan campus—he isn't there for any reason Harry can discern—perhaps doing obligatory facetime at the University to satisfy his employer and obviate some legal issue.

In the college winter of cloistered and overheated Midwest rooms, Harry sweats. A lot. In the presence of people who might want something from him. Rooted to the spot, sunk like a seed poked by a giant finger into the soil. He imagines himself in a pool of mucky earth that he is melting into.

Snowbound in the dorms. Occasional unwelcome knocks on the

door—a dorm neighbor wants Harry to join the hall party—Harry sits still and quiet in his room. A knock comes late. He doesn't get up to answer until he hears: "Harry. Bash-man's about froze to death. Wanna let me in?"

Basher, coated in a layer of fine mist, his khaki cuffs soaked. No jacket, just layers of work shirts. An old wool cap like a farmer would wear cantilevered out at each side with drawstrings, over his ears, cradling puffs of snow.

"I'm walking around. Beautiful night. Thought you might be sulking over here, Harry. Can't drink this stuff all by myself."

His rebellious, "conservative" hippie look complete with dark frame glasses. Cultivated nonchalance. His arm crooks strangely, protected from view. Basher shrugs. "I was waiting for someone forever at the Union. Thought I'd put myself to use shoveling the walk. What a smacker." Basher holds up a brown sacked bottle with his good arm. "The night guard felt sorry for me. The buses stopped running."

An iceberg coming slowly through a room, people get out of Harry's way. Except for Basher. Basher seems to stick around for Harry, or come back to him, as if attending to the iceberg that is Harry. Basher puts him in his pocket and takes him out as if Harry were unaccountable to his own misery.

Basher begins stripping down to long johns mis-washed to a shade of lavender and a ripped, worn white t-shirt that reads *University of Manitoba*, like a sign to the next available exit.

"Do you mind if I put these here?"

Harry nods, uncommitted to a fault.

Basher schematically arranges these pieces the way he would wet photographic paper, across the table in front of the radiator.

"Don't worry. I like you, Harry." Basher guffaws. "Not *that* much." Teases the idea. "Or maybe just." Hoisting the bottle, he says, "You got some glasses?"

Harry drinks fast. The wine is good. Warm and slightly viscid and a bit bloodlike in his throat. With all the snow, he can forget studying for his *Ethics and Responsibility in the Media* test tomorrow.

For most of the last month Basher had talked about his job based in Paris like it was no big deal: the world at his dirty fingertips. Harry is glad for Basher's company, but will not admit it now. He wants to enter into that lucid space of his friend's, still, he can't do it yet, can't feel it, really.

Basher sits on the bed. Harry stays placid, passive, at his desk. "Sit," Basher pats the twin bed, mildly. "Over here."

Harry gets up and moves as if by gravitational force, lumbering, wine thrumming in his veins, and sits down next to Basher. Basher leans back, tipping, slow. He draws him near, without comment. Harry can smell him—something Harry only notices unconsciously. His foot searches for the bottle and cups he knows are there to be crushed underfoot. The bottle falls and thumps with a clink against the metal leg of the bed.

They are drunk. Basher's tapping hand on his shoulder. An easy lifting of Harry's t-shirt. Like his father undressing him when he was a boy. He could do it himself, but he was lazy and lethargic and had a reason then. Basher's cool hands now along his sides. It tickles, and he suppresses a nervous, braying laugh and looks toward the door.

"You locked it," Basher says.

In later recollection, amid the stale cigarette breath and tannin wine Harry would explain his behavior—his complicity—by convincing himself that Basher had slipped him drugs.

*Item:* At a Halloween party Harry, dressed as a garbage man in blue coveralls, with a skull cap and charcoal grimed face—they thought he was trying to go as a criminal—remembered walking into Basher's friend's house (absent Basher) and seeing a jaguar, a serpent and a nurse, their faces dusted like baker's apprentices with cocaine piles on the glass table. Some odd energy there, a triangle in the process of revealing itself; these were Basher's wild friends, was Harry's incoherence. Their pale blue faces iridescent in the shadowy living room. Basher's world, he thought.

He forgets how it transpires. Basher has done this before. He has drawn Harry along into this society. Harry, wanting to show his worth, his sense of appreciation, grips Basher awkwardly back.

When he falls into the embrace it is as if he has missed out on it in life. Suddenly he is a child in his mother's arms again, clinging onto her in sheer desperation because mother will take care of you *forever*. When all along he knows soon enough, at any moment she will be gone, *forever*.

Harry hasn't even had a girlfriend yet. He's met some girls, and made out with some, but they never stay around. He doesn't know how to get them to. He tries, hard. No luck.

Basher has been with girls, a known fact. With women. Maybe there were other guys for all Harry knows. But there are definitely women. Basher is nothing if not opportunistic. He lives in Paris.

Harry thinks, *They're going to think we're queers*, because he knows they already think this about Basher. Now Harry conflates Basher's queerness with his own iceberg-ness. Something inside, a destiny. Basher's odd-ness.

Thinking about himself as a seducer—however unlikely—trying

to displace Basher's power over him, Harry says, "So that's how the foot feels in a different shoe?"

Basher laughs. "What you mean, I think, is how the shoe fits on the other foot."

Basher performs to his audience of one: Harry, malleable, ungrounded, feeling like that metal from another planet that weighs so much that it falls right through the earth; what Harry had always wondered was how they could figure out that it weighed so much. Ignoble metal.

Basher's yellow fingers with their cracked acid ridges, the hay-ey breath that Harry calls horehound because it correlates with an idea of the word. *Whore-hound*. Basher's breath, disgusting, really, has an unusual effect on him—the way he sometimes feels drawn inexplicably to stink.

He imagines he (Harry) is in love with him—or, Basher is in love with him. Or seducing him.

He has obsessed himself with this for awhile—since two winters ago.

Basher confuses. He mocks. He terrorizes. Harry is curious to know more of him. To keep hold of him. Harry wonders where it is going, and won't fight it. He's bored with Basher gone. Basher returns and gives him attention.

Still, no one need ever know, which is good.

Because everything with Basher is a jumping off point; Harry doesn't know what comes next.

Basher says, "I love you," and the world settles down like a sheet around him.

Twisting around in wrinkled blankets in the December cold in the glare of the streetlamp through the dorm window, I love you. The words make him quiver, overcome. Crying.

"Oh gee," Basher says, conveniently misreading him. "I don't have to stay, you know."

Buried under blankets with his friend, holding onto him through that night. Harry'd either wanted it to last forever or just have it end instantly. But what he learned then is what he has carried into adulthood. No matter how much you want someone—to be like them—no matter how much you let yourself go for them, it is never enough. You will always suffer and fall under for that feeling, and it will always make you pay. Someday they are gone. Into the ether.

As if to deny it all, to defuse it from his thoughts, in the midst of this woozy and weird camaraderie, Basher switches gears. "Guess what? I quit smoking."

Harry dozes. He does not know for how long. After he awakes, he starts thinking again. Restless, like he has been trying to wake himself up the whole time to remind himself of an urgency. He dreamt that he was hanging on to the rail of a small aluminum boat like the one he used to have to beg his father to take out from the barn (as if it were some great inconvenience—the boat, left there from the previous owner, sat barricaded behind the season's leftover, moldering hay bales). He couldn't let go. He awakes in the cold night clutching his chilled left side, the boat bed is sinking, unpleasantly damp from his sweat. *Their* sweat? Basher holds the covers. Harry tugs at them. Above Basher, Harry sees the street lights making crystal doilies on the frozen window. He'll never get back to sleep now.

The radiator wrenches and hisses. The room is a descending submarine with a porthole sized view onto the last gray wastes of his life, the sleeping quad, a ring of spiky frost framing all. His friend snores unimpeded, a pressure in his brain. Uncontrollable rage. Defeat. He is small in that skiff of a bed, sharing it. He kicks Basher so hard and regrets it, and tenses up for the expected return kick. But Basher turns away from the wall, snuffs loudly and releases some of the fugitive covers.

Just before the holiday break, Harry keeps his eyes open for Basher around campus, characteristically absent. Avoiding him. Harry pretends to do the same.

It was like Basher was playing with him. Once or twice they might have happened to cross paths at the student union. As was usually the case, Harry saw his friend with someone compelling Harry'd not have the nerve to ingratiate himself to, and certainly not in light of what had happened a few weeks earlier. Harry notices Basher from a distance, across the Diag, or, he sees Basher being corralled by a professor or an envious classmate. He shadows them like a sniper for the length of a block until they duck into a building.

In the library, Harry flinches when he spots him. Surprise attack. Basher is dressed neat and immaculate in a button down shirt and tie. Wool pants and buckskin loafers. Combed hair. Cleaned up for some important interview—the press bureaus all courting him now. Harry speculates and projects from a safe distance most of the time, hoping he isn't seen.

He knows enough to not try to read his friend, because he recalls how Basher has confided a professional impassivity that guides his life. *How you act on a job—can't reveal emotions. Can't get involved. It's not about you out there.* Basher had taken him into the darkroom to show him how he had burned in the ominous details of a washed out sky for dramatic effect. Or better, how the character of a face that he forgot he had captured on film was slowly revealed in the developing bath on a piece of photographic paper. The face in its harsh tortured expression, suddenly revealing subtle nuances in the bland light of the darkroom.

Harry watches Basher, and waits for acknowledgment. Basher is in turn waiting for someone. His face at these times might as well be a blank.

Yet, as soon as Basher sees him, he is upon Harry's table.

As if Harry were an irrelevant border guard that Basher has to negotiate past, a formality, Basher calmly turns the cover to look at Harry's book. "Ethics and Responsibility in the Media?" Basher snorts. "So beside the point."

Rage emanates and spreads like a force field around Harry. He slams his book shut. Basher walks away without a word.

# III. MATERIAL

*Which is often like saying it did not happen the way that it happened, that this was not a child, this was not land bleeding under oppression, this was not a foreign country rife with militias and children wandering coke eyed through dusty fields with gerry-rigged Kalashnikovs. It is like saying the event had a higher purpose, ascribing meaning to an action that so irrevocably, so suddenly, so certainly, and so unlikely, took a life often misguided, but generally well-intentioned. Tell that to his mother, was often the phrase heard about this meaningless act with so much meaning carried in it. Meaning that, it had no purpose other than the point of saying what it meant was not what anyone talked about meant it to mean (in muted tones around his mother, that summer, the first months after it happened, that first year), but that some hazy eyed, green handed child of this third world underworld, had meant to fire the adult's weapon, had understood that his act would extend and arc and fork into a future of lives he could never comprehend and thus reverberate beyond what he meant, which was likely not meant to mean a damn thing. Meaning his friend's mother had to forgive, had to make amends when she returned with his ashes, had to find a meaning where there was no meaning.*

**Cassette tape with handwritten label, "Radio show 1974."**

Harry runs his finger across the buttons of the tape deck, pushing a pinch of brown dust between his fingers. He presses play. An old tape.

[A rhine of smooth wheels across asphalt. Clicks. Hiss and pop.]

"I'm suppos'to answer a question."

Basher's confident tone, somehow detached.

"Wait!"

[Tape static. Rumbles. Clicks.]

"How do I?"

". . . s easy enough. Usually I just get them . . . and then I won't be looking. No. That's right. I won't look. It makes . . . and then people are unaware."

[Drop outs. Pops.]

Deteriorating magnetic tape.

"Come on . . . How do you do that?"

Harry, with dismay, notes his own fey, wispy child's voice.

"I just hold out my camera and take the picture. When you—"

Harry clicked off the tape. Popped it out and looked at it again. His own handwriting. He'd hardly remembered sitting in the cold attic room playing reporter with Basher. Setting up semi-elaborate radio programs based on their exclusive knowledge of the world. He put the tape back in.

"—do it nonchalantly. You know."

"Wait. Is that a fancy word or something?"

"What?"

"That word . . . Nonshollonty . . . What's'at mean?"

"Non-chalantly. French. So no one pays any attention."

"Really?"

"Yes."

"Okay."

"What did you want to ask me?"

"I don't know."

[Riffling of pages. Tape hiss and pause. Static whir. Tape clicks.]

" . . . *ahhhhn ahhhhn ahhhhn ahhhhn ahhhhhhhhhhhhhhh* . . . "

Three seconds of a once familiar song, distorted, the recording level excessively high.

[Tape clicks two times.]

"Do you have anything important to say to the . . . to . . . the . . . American public?"

"It's a dangerous job, but someone has to do it."

"What exactly is it that's so dangerous?"

"What do you mean? . . . *What* is dangerous?"

"Yeah."

"Well, let's see. You have to be there, you know, where the shooting is happening."

"I see . . . Okay . . . Tell us then, what you did in Hanoi."

"Hmmmm . . . I did . . . I didn't . . . I did. I didn't say to ask about Hanoi."

"Wait! I thought you said."

"Oh. Hold on. I know . . . You have to sto . . . Har . . . Stop!"

[Tape clicks. Hiss.]

*". . . omma said the way you mooove, gonna make you sweat, gonna make you grooooove . . ."*

Several seconds of music. Abrupt.

[More clicks.]

"Okay, then. Now . . . Tell us about youth in Asia."

"About what?"

"Youth in Asia."

"Euthanasia?"

"Mmmmm . . . Yeah."

"Why?"

"It's interesting . . . Tell us . . . Why we should care about 'youth in Asia'?"

[Basher laughing.]

Trying not to. Embarrassing.

"Why don't . . . why . . . don't you tell me . . ."

[Tape clicks.]

"Hold up . . . Harry . . . is the tape running?"

"Yeah."

"I have to think about this."

"What."

"I want to rehearse, man! Let's work on this later."

"Okay."

Agreeable.

"Besides, I'm getting kinda thirsty."

"Yeah."

"Do you wanna bike to the store?"

"Sure."

"Let's go."

[Tape clicks.]

"*mnnnmnn . . . mnnnn . . . mmnn . . . mmnnnnnn . . .*"

Jimmy Page's frantic guitar solo. A few seconds.

[Tape clicks.]

"Ready now?"

"Let's see . . . Umm . . . I . . . Here. Tell us about your meeting with . . . Tricky Dick!"

[Quick laughs.]

Nervous.

"Oh yes."

Basher with haughty, affected self-importance.

"Let me see . . . I was a guest at the White House. You know. My father is old friends with him."

"No way."

"Well, yeah . . . Of course."

"What's he call him?"

"Oh, you know . . ."

Basher's deep and affected nasally tone.

"Ahem . . . Meeeester President."

[They laugh, stop with a snort.]

Trying to sound artificially professional.

[Pause and hiss of tape.]

"Not . . . Dicky?"

[Laughter]

Out of control.

[Wheels whistling. Repeated tape clicks. Music comes in abruptly.]

". . . eyes that shine . . . a' burning red . . . dreams of you all thru my head . . ."

[Tape clicks.]

In the clear light, the landmasses in plates of earthtone color, the satellite maps clearly show Baja, what he could remember from those empty roads.

On the computer Harry'd get lost for hours on United States Geological Survey maps, setting it to satellite view once he'd found the road, then the town, Mulege, the road a black crack through a hollow eyed desert.

He lugs the box into the library and, to be less obvious, lays some of the photographs out on a table far in the back behind the stacks. Here, he doesn't have to explain his research to Janelle.

Harry studies The U.S.G.S. high resolution satellite photographs. The photographs, in a computer database, are a guide to his own memories for tracking the landscapes he knew vaguely (Baja), and some he'd imagine based on Basher's photographs, and from notes encrypted on the back of proof sheets from the archival box. He inspects long aerial views, focusing in on a smaller and smaller square of land. Increasing the resolution to where he discerns the man-made scars amid vast tracts of empty desert: roofs, habitable structures, roads. Trying to find a single barely discernible sand colored road jutting off the trans-peninsula highway into the barren moonscape of Baja. He could not remember the names of most of the small towns after where they had set up camp near the Sea of Cortez, aka, the Gulf of California. Those towns were so small, the roads indistinguishable, without names, unmarked.

He recognizes the grid of Santa Rosalia and remembers the white iron church designed by Gustav Eiffel meant to be a prototype prefab metal church for a French colony in Africa, undelivered. The simple, impressively plain gothic façade, like an oxymoron, stood at the entry to the town.

He focuses in on the coastline looking for their beach and zooming out, he scans a fragment of the landscape, perhaps a few miles from that beach. Like the drive in the car, not being able to see the overall plan or to discern land forms that altered relative to the perspective. In motion, shape and boundary constantly shifted. He recognizes the knife edge strip of beach along the rocky coast curving out into an odd mound of earth off the Gulf of California.

The door on Basher's world opened up on the trip to Baja. Harry, for the first time in his life, found himself clean in the middle of nowhere—or what felt like nowhere, with Basher's emphasized, "You can imagine there's nothing around here for a thousand miles. It's like the Pamir Mountains." Of the myriad other places Harry might never make it to that Basher explored (Tajikistan). Basher's field. Baja was desolate, more desolate than the Northern towns Harry knew of in Michigan, nothing seemed to have taken hold there.

The desolation.

Maybe this is what drew him to Baja.

Most of the tales revolved around the incidental, but Harry had always suspected this was to cover up the ample and terrifying photographic evidence.

Basher had been trained to keep his distance from it, perhaps becoming desensitized to document misery. He saw it so frequently that it must have left its trace. He didn't admit fear, and talked matter of factly about the blasted limbs, the bloodied hands, the charred concrete. Crumbled walls, bullet pocked, painted red, obliterated by sand, wind and sea. A rusting ferry crossing a milk coffee river uncoiling through an impenetrable jungle. Walking for miles through unfamiliar cities to find the site of crimes against humanity. What might eventually be raked, turned, effaced, built over, built upon, removed.

Still, when asked, Basher talked about having been up to his knees in a mass grave in Zimbabwe. He took a panoramic shot in granular black and white to emphasize the horror, the infinite sky so bright it burned the eyes. The earth dissolving skin and the sun bleaching the bones. So many bones, he said, an abstraction; if you don't recognize the forms, what can make you weep? He became sanguine. The damage was done. His work became an opportunity to open the eyes of the world.

His pictures lifted unaccountable events from their ignominy, and aficionados would study the compositions for their aesthetics. *You see,* Basher once told him, *as much as I want to scream and yell, I know the worst is always yet to come. It's the endless plain of fortune.*

Harry could never experience those places the same way now, even if he wanted to. The world had changed too fast. He satisfied himself with the long view. He turned to the satellite photos to explain it all. He would work from the images, translate those into words, reconfiguring the words to make another object to stop time.

A mind numbing repetition of images were the proof sheets. They indicated what Basher's eyes had witnessed firsthand and would not be acceptable to the popular press. Even the idea that he had been bold enough to take the pictures, that the victim or those who narrowly missed the attack would not feel indignation, violation, at the sight of the camera.

The benign, even the artful images—if a body transformed by a civil war could be called artful—to Harry's trained eyes, are crossed out with a giant felt tip X editorially across them, forever relegating a unique image to the emptiness and sovereignty of its origin. To Harry, there is a disturbing negation to the photos with the ink X that lays the ultimate critique on it. When he looks through the negative sheets, he can never discern the original. But he can see the series in the magazines, and guesses at the locations.

He pores through old copies of *Time* and *Life*, and connects the pictures with the credits to the stories Basher had told him. Because the story in the press was rarely the one behind the photographer's words, which was often the technical side of things, unfiltered and unmediated. When someone said something their face didn't lie, and the reporter who jotted down the story may or may not use the quote later. But Basher had witnessed truth. The wear and tear of the facades, he'd called it. The endless plain of fortune.

## Carbon copy of letter. April, 1981

Harry is surprised to learn that the letters from his friend were often duplicates that he sent to everyone.

Harry read the letter and it was déjà vu.

As I like to say, I'm a non-partial spectator -- actually, I don't like that word -- I'm non-involved. Bullets aren't partial. I'm not supposed to be. Sometimes I get into trouble when I take too much of a personal stand.

Recently, I was in this village along the Niger. They have me at this outpost -- the bureau does -- for the second time. I've been set up in a hut with some "bodyguards". Local fellows, and to be honest I'm not sure I am any more safe at all. You have to wonder, why the bodyguards in the first place?

I'm in the market that day taking pictures of a meeting between the tribal leader and the government puppet, the signing of an important treaty.

Nothing comes out of the first meeting. It's a picture perfect stalemate. All the factions involved fumble with their little folders of papers, looking around, checking the clock, whatever, dreaming of lunch. So, everyone tosses up their hands and backs away to their corners to scheme for the next meeting, and I go back to my hut to take a nap, maybe for twenty minutes (recovering from jet lag). I start hearing these eerie cries which I guess might have been singing, except it's not the kind of singing with drums that you expect to hear.

Tribal music doesn't usually give me the jim-jams, but there's a distinct sinister note to it this time. Coupled with the bird-like ululations and you've got one sleepless siesta. Not being one to sit idle, I decide to go investigate.

My guards, whom I don't even get to know by name -- an oversight on my part, really -- are waiting to discuss an important matter with me.

I have a sense about this diversion. They are all talking trying to warn me of something, I'm sure, but no one is making any sense. "He left on a motorcycle." "It was a woman, she was here." "You have a message, sir, but we have to leave right away."

I figure I'll go with it, something live going down, perhaps. I duck back in to the hut and the camera bag I've literally slept with since checking into my red-eye

-- there was some reason I clung to that thing like my personal flotation device -- has walked away.

I come out of the tent and they start telling me they chased this guy for a bit, someone who had been poking around in my hut while I was sleeping. They followed him through the market, down an alley, until he got on a motorcycle and took off.

Later, it's all down time at the village. One of my guides (I've ceased to think of them as guards by now) walks me over to a stand where everyone congregates -- beer, palm wine.

That night villagers are coming up to me with hot tips or advice. I can find your bag, they say. More confusion, innuendo. It happens more than once. They take me on these wild goose chases through the village. We end up back at the cantina and the fellow admits to me that he doesn't know exactly where the camera bag is, but that he might know someone who does, and he will take me there for a small token of appreciation. I am getting annoyed but play along, though I have written the camera bag off. I have insurance. Still, I'm not keen for my boss to catch me in the middle of this story without my tools, it's so early in my career.

So, this night I'm outside at the cantina and a young girl approaches me. She says, "Sa Thomas, I know where to find your bag." She said, "First you have to give me twenty cowries." No thanks, I say. Everyone is in on this, I tell the girl, and there will be hell to pay. I say within earshot of the curious that it is wrong for anyone to take advantage of a stranger -- especially someone who is there on their behalf, yours truly. No one seems to understand me, they just smile. Unimpressed.

I decide to contact Rand and explain the predicament. I have to leave the next day anyway. But the little adventure isn't over yet.

Enter the Goddess Mother -- that's what we call her, a kind of sage there -- everyone looks up to her. The crowd literally parts when this woman is present. We had had an unusual confrontation once before, and I never understood what her proverbs were about. This time, she says, "Remember, Sa Thomas, the hawk may fly to the serpent, but the serpent does not always fly away."

I guess you could say the Goddess Mother enlightened me.

She wanted it to be known that the new government was oppressing the village, and it was suggested that, more importantly than my taking their souls, I should take a message to the government. In other words, I should not take any more pictures of the people and I would get my cameras back. I had to promise to keep the cameras home next time, which was, at that moment for me, a total absurdity. I lied as best I could, thinking I would be hard pressed to explain my purpose there to anyone.

Later that night, my bag reappeared in the tent. Cameras intact.

Apparently, I had made the mistake of once having shown the Goddess Mother some of the pictures on a contact proof -- from a set I had taken on the earlier visit.

When she saw these pictures, she was silent and stopped speaking to me. In awe of the work, or so I thought.

The question that bugged me for the longest time is: am I the hawk, or the serpent?

I never went back.

Basher had many occasions of stolen cameras. On one of his trips across Europe on the Orient Express (so called), he had fallen asleep in the wrong compartment to awake the next morning to a nearly empty train with his backpack gone. It had been a crowded train, and his compartment was taken over by some old men talking, he figured they were Turkish, with the obligatory fez and monocle, he'd said (perhaps he was joking) and he thought, one compartment over was a space where everyone was quiet so he went there to get some sleep. When he awoke, dawn had broken and he was greeted by the minarets of Istanbul, reminding him of ballistic missiles.

    The conductor saw him and knew, led him without a word through three cars into the lavatory of the last car where his bag lay out like a botched surgery. Spilled open, its guts on the lavatory floor for all to stomp on. Basher dropped to his knees, soaking them on the wet floor, sifted through this pile (it was before he knew there was insurance on his gear) and dug in frantically—no, he said he wasn't so interested in what had happened to the cameras, at that moment, he was more interested in finding the film. The camera was gone, but the rolls of film he'd shot in rural China were there. These were pictures he'd later win the Prix Nadar for, and he always credited the thieves with his success. He never mentioned if the cameras ever turned up.

Harry lifts the photograph to study.

Two figures on a bank. No names given but the undeniable recognition. Reading the word *Adriatic* penciled in cursive on the back of photos that were from the same set, dated June, 1981. The same place. He could smell the Adriatic summer. Another of Basher's haunts he'd never been. A sand spit of beach and the burn of light on a needle of Southern water.

Green, her top, yellow summer skirt with repeating figures, clenched around her knees. Basher, cut offs and no shirt. That static electrified hair. More hair than he'd remembered. Definitely young. The photograph's deception? As if only in his mind Basher should appear old then because he was like an older figure in Harry's life. But here he was, stuck in acetate, the last images. Basher and a familiar woman.

He hadn't thought about her in over twenty years.

They were lovers.

Anyone could gather this much.

Harry didn't think that he had gotten there for seconds. Sloppy seconds as boys are wont to say.

The summer heat you can taste in the sea air and the breeze lilting their wild hair. To wonder whose eyes are the eyes that stood before them, framed the scene, and took the picture. His arm around her shoulders. She looks about to slip off the rock they are precariously gripping with their bare feet. As if the light is undiminished two decades on, a blaze of bleached summer heat making a penumbra of their forms. She leans and angles her body, magnetized to Basher who props her with his encircling arm. Christiane, minus messy reality, lighter hair than he had remembered her North African blood—she's Algerian—having fixed in his memory, that impenetrable ink black hair that captured light, not a shadowy smear. Not this young hair. Not as interesting on this evidence, minus messy reality.

Not so interesting because she was younger then? Or not so interesting because in the picture she was not yet his—Harry's—if she ever was. In the photo, she is clearly Basher's. Not so interesting because since then she had come and gone from Harry's life.

They look younger than he remembers feeling then. Basher could not have known her for too long before Baja.

Their destination is an empty secluded beach with miles of dunes that Basher had come to before in his Volkswagen van. Empty because as yet, largely undiscovered. Basher idealizes the 1500 mile journey. "You watch," Basher says. "In a few years, desolation beach," (as he called it) "will be overrun with Hollywood studio bosses' summer homes."

They stop long enough for Jarrito's Cola and Pacifico. Harry sits next to Christiane while Basher drives with Big Bob in the passenger seat. Harry has brought his reading with him to study, and makes a first self-conscious attempt to document real life. Writing of the trip he tries to conjure precision and a near miss poetical inspiration. When they stop he lets Basher read a few snippets. Doggerel, Harry fears. Basher closes his eyes after he reads as if to gather the storm force of Harry's words:

> *red dirt roads foreground*
> *huddled blue hills*
> *an orgy of*

*sleeping figures*

*shot blue powder*

*earnest sky*

"You hate it," Harry suggests.

"Harry, I didn't say anything."

Harry ignores Basher's growing photojournalism career. Out of self-preservation, to avoid jealousy. It's bad enough for him as it is.

Basher is captain of a ship that they are all merely passengers on. Basher is too pleased with himself. How unfair that he'd arrived there, was always and as yet still arriving somewhere, miraculous, unencumbered. Worst of all is recognizing it: Harry's burden. Big Bob Devine is along for the ride, smoking too many cigarettes. The presence of Christiane, somehow at odds with Basher, seems like an aspiration. She wears a perfume that makes Harry think about earnest skies above the Mediterranean sea.

As they stand outside the supermercado, Basher confesses to Harry.

"I shouldn't have brought her."

It's quiet out, but for a roadside bodega, where border radio snakes out from the smoky, fluorescent bright interior. The four gauchos in there are playing a card game. It's possibly three in the morning. Harry looks up into the sky and sees the spider claws of Orion, like a web being cast over the edge of Baja.

Basher looks for lodgings.

He drives the car through a concrete portal, entering a courtyard. They get two rooms at the pink walled motel, one for Christiane and one for the three men. Like all of the buildings here, it is concrete and cinder blocks, with a shallow sloped roof on which rebar stanchions stick up at the edges for a structurally dubious, if optimistic, future addition. The walls are glistening with moisture. All night the trucks pass like somnambulistic phantoms through the muddy roadways, creaking and stalling trying to make their way to the resorts of Cabo. The misty air is fragrant from the evaporating sea and fog spills across neon lit signs and films the bright glass window fronts. The towns do not seem to sleep, but are merely sleepy, and remind Harry of the truck stops along the interstates back home, catering to the sporadic, ever wide awake distribution of domestic wares and automobile parts. An occasional car without lights, hung low on its bowed chassis, skitters recklessly down the highway.

Basher waits behind Harry at the door to the room and then goes back to the van for something. Harry turns the key several times to get the knob to unlock, shoulders hard the door as he wrenches the knob. He hits the lights. The bulb buzzes like a winter fly. The room is as bright as the sunlit day. He looks up at the ceiling which bubbles with condensed water. Water fills half the light bulb. As if he senses this is the only option, he wades into the room pooled with a half inch of standing water. The last available motel room in the town. He touches the bedspread, just to be sure it is dry, only to feel it soaked. The bed is a sponge.

The water laps and splashes off the walls. A drop smacks him cold in the ear.

The three men reconnoiter to sleep in tortured postures in the van in the parking lot of the motel.

In the morning, Christiane awakes them with a knock on the window.

Basher lands on the brakes when some dun colored cows position themselves en masse on the road. Harry and Christiane slide forward, their faces pressing into the seats ahead of them. Big Bob crouches into the floorboards cradling his beers while Basher holds himself athwart the steering wheel like he's commandeering an immense tanker, taking it off the road at the last moment. After bottoming the van out in a vado, down through a rocky ditch and up onto the desert scrub, he keeps driving in lazy S curves. Cacti and slipper plants rake under the chassis as they hump over boulders. As the van rolls to a stop he jumps out to survey the landscape in the high beams.

 They sit outside along the highway as trucks rumble by every few minutes; first painting a long cast of distant headlights on them. Basher, walking into the darkness with a penlight to gather sticks for the fire, diminishes to a point of faint light. Harry trails along, halfway between Basher and the van, keeping in sight of the van's dim dome light, cold in his long sleeve shirt and the extra sweater pulled from a thrift pile in the back of the van. Big Bob dispatches three beers and chains cigarettes while sitting with his back against the van, occasionally tooting on his harmonica. Christiane walks toward the road, alone. Basher seems to be brokering a disastrous negotiation with her, Harry thinks, but he does not ask.

 He can hear in the dark Big Bob dragging from the van one of Basher's smelly German Army tents ("They're not like anything else,") the laborious erecting and climbing in and finally hunkering down to sleep. In minutes, his rasping, projected snore is punctuated by moments of coughing and stirring.

 "We're going to have to rough it. Christiane won't put up with snoring."

Basher enjoys telling Harry the story of his relationship with Christiane. How, when he first met her she recounted to him all the ways they would have met, because she was already idealizing and projecting. He used a French accent and imitated her. Just sink, if you vould have been born in Paris, he said she said.

"This is when she thought she had me," Basher says. "You know what I mean? Like I was going to fall into her trap."

Basher called her a *bourgeois*. Basher said that Christiane had said it was tragic that he was not French, as if this were even possible, and how they could have met sooner.

"We would have been toast much sooner," Basher said.

This seems unnecessarily cruel; he can't tell the source of Basher's mockery, the motivation.

He decides she's hurt him.

Basher is vulnerable!

Harry considers Basher is giving her away, as odd as this seems.

"Why did she come then?" Harry asks.

"Long story."

Christiane had come to see in Basher someone slightly less refined than he was—Basher told Harry this much with a laugh. As if she was too classy for him.

Harry sees a new facet of Basher, forgets it almost as soon. He would always see Basher in a new light, a light that then shines on himself, however dubiously and calculating, perhaps, and so Harry only wonders, If she's too classy for you, what about me?

Christiane, like many of Basher's women, has a certitude that is intolerable to Basher, because it matches his bravado—in essence, it cancels him out. This only makes Christiane grow in Harry's eyes. After spending hours in the back of the van with her, Harry doesn't give a damn about the bourgeoisie. He is enchanted by this woman, ready to jump.

Christiane reminds Harry of a girl in school that he always finds attractive but whom most of the guys ignore because she is what they call unusual looking. Meaning: not from here. He likes the foreigners, the exchange students, they are friendly up to a limit but they are often maddeningly aloof.

It might be wise to not get involved.

On his early morning jog down the beach, Harry swears he sees the banditos—two dark figures in bedouin garb—black shrouds, floating and peering from behind a sand dune. They move so as to let him know they are watching him and don't expect him to linger or come looking for them, which is true enough. The others will never believe his eyewitness account; he can hear Basher's mockery in his head. The banditos are a symbol of your fear, he'll be sure to say. Harry thinks these despairing thoughts while wading in the water. In another time, he imagines, in some future, he might actually enjoy this memory because at one time he will recall it made him feel alive, but he can't right now. He struggles to get beyond the grip of his fear, fetters that bind him to his woe like a penitent.

He hopes Christiane is beginning to see in him something that he cannot yet see in himself, and he is ready to believe it, ready to let the springs fly off. He craves the illusion. How he is ready to let go and damn his doubts anyway.

Basher and Christiane are ambiguous in their dealings with each other, and Harry can learn nothing from the apparently telltale fact that they share a tent the first two days in Baja. They are far enough away, but he can hear them arguing. They keep it between them. It's only a matter of time with Basher's veiled ambivalence, almost painful to witness. He senses in Christiane's turbulent manner with Basher a final fallout.

Basher grabs his surf board, Christiane sits alone on the beach reading a tattered newspaper in Arabic. A knowledgeable look on her face. The first brief gesture toward Harry, when she lifts her Jackie O. sunglasses and looks searchingly into his eyes, offers a lingering touch on his arm. Watch out for her, Harry. She'll eat you alive. She looks as if she could walk down Fifth Avenue in those boots, a calfskin number.

There is another spat, brief and silent. Basher walks away, flailing his arms around in a kind of jokey frustration. Christiane's movement says, don't follow me. Harry wants to inquire. He isn't that bold; not yet anyway. Their relationship is none of his business if he ever wants anything further to do with her. Or Basher. He watches her march off to the east horizon in her boots with her leather satchel slung over her shoulder, wonders where she's going. She becomes a shimmering cursor on the chaparral's flat screen, her form stretches vertically on the mirage of sunburned desert. He hopes she won't get lost. Basher notices Harry's concern, reassures him

"Don't sweat it, Harry. She's got more balls than you and I put together."

The three men sit on the beach.

Big Bob offers, "Gone shopping."

The figures he had seen on the hills earlier that morning Harry thinks of as an omen.

Harry stands at the edge of the water as Basher's naked buttocks streak by. Basher dashes far out and drops into the water, waving his arms at him. Harry, noting that Christiane has not returned, chucks his shorts onto the beach and runs in. Big Bob stays on the sand digging a moat around his ad hoc sand castle. Before Harry has been two minutes in the water, he looks back at the beach. Christiane stands over Big Bob's castle. She waves to them.

She might have caught a glimpse of his ass. And more. The thought gives him the stirring of an erection.

A jet cuts across the sun and high banks of drifting clouds, and a shadow sweeps over the water, their isolated corner of civilization, and it's as if a giant hand is passing overhead, settling wearily on him.

Something pinches his leg.

It takes all of his strength to run through the shallow water and get to the beach. The sting is so searing he is sure he is going to die. He whines on the trundle to safety. But it hurts. "They got you," Basher calls out calmly, as if it is an initiation. Basher means to be lighthearted about it and tries to grab Harry by the arm, to guide him, but Harry shrugs him off. All of his caution is for nothing. He stands naked before them, covers himself with his hands and looks up to see Christiane's face, reflecting his own, a look of concern, worry. A moment of relief. She walks toward him and hands him a towel.

"Sea jellies," Basher's running commentary begins. "They shock your nervous system—you'll be tired soon. I should have noticed them. They drift in these massive clouds out there, you can't see them till they're all that surrounds you."

Harry shakes. The bolt of the sting draws his adrenaline, makes him nauseous. He has no idea if Basher talks to annoy him or because he thinks it will keep Harry calm.

Basher tosses him a bottle of aspirin.

Harry takes three and finishes off the water jug that Christiane hands him.

Basher, still naked, thankfully grabs a towel and puts it around his waist.

"I can see those damn things from here," Bob says.

Christiane gets up to run back to the tents for more water.

She takes care of things.

Harry leans back onto the towel and closes his eyes. He wants to fall into the arms of this woman, he just wants to take a chance. He knows he has to play his sea-jelly-sting right, so that he doesn't come out of it looking like a complete wuss.

The feeling comes back to his leg, cold turns to tingling. Bob brings a warm bottle of Pacifico, pops it open and pushes it into the sand in front of Harry before he walks to the water and stabs at the sand with his stick.

Christiane's heart stopping scream makes the hair on the back of his neck prickle.

He sits up.

Basher runs toward the tents. Ridiculous and chivalrous Basher crests the hill, towel barely hanging onto his knobby hips.

The tents ransacked, they assess what has been stolen. Some pesos, two shirts, a sleeping bag. Basher luckily kept the keys for the van in his shoe.

There is a chemical attraction between them, Harry is convinced.

He isn't sure he could offer her anything. They've begun to talk.

Her voice, the words in their jagged roll through the tent, telling stories he gets caught up in, how she feels alone in the world, wants to find love, all that. Her sadness, a melancholy; he has it, also. They will hover around each other with this private understanding. She tells him about her life in Paris. An intoxication. A ferris wheel.

Falling off the consonants of her voice—each time it catches him and lets him drop again and again and again.

He weighs the idea that sitting in the tent with her now might really get to Basher. If it even troubles Basher, to say the least, this sense of Harry pursuing the woman Basher brought to him. It is possible Harry does it to provoke him, Basher, who cannot be provoked. Basher so much a mountain unto himself that he doesn't need anyone, which is what he more or less says, which is what Harry always believes about him.

Harry becomes Christiane's confessor. He isn't the best audience for this.

Basher might turn against her even more now, as Harry moves in. She complains of Basher. Harry tries to be compassionate. Then, frustrated at having to take sides, he says, "We all think we are at fault."

"I thought you'd say that," she says, disappointed, looking away.

The ice of the December wind slips through the tent, the smell of smoke from the fire. Avoid defeat, Harry reminds himself. Go forward.

He backpedals. "I just meant."

It is her way. He shouldn't feel a need to explain. She makes gestures, acknowledges his being the third point on the triangle, lets him in. He feels bold, wants to ask her where she goes on those walks alone for hours, and how he'd like to take that walk with her, tomorrow.

She reaches out and touches his neck. He places his hand,

awkwardly, on her leg. Too late. She doesn't move it. She doesn't want to talk anymore. She leans on him, embraces him.

"Just hold me," she says. The bottom falling out.

He wants more, too. He tells her.

"Maybe if you come to Paris," she suggests. Her voice comforting in the dark.

They lie down early and through the tent's netting watch the campfire burn out. In the tent, cavernous as an igloo and as cold, he has a raging headache from the smoke, but she wraps her arms around him, rubs his temples and kisses him, gives him one of her French prescription migraine pills. In the pitch black beneath their zippered together sleeping bags she goes down on him. This is a gift. In the dark, he thinks, she won't be embarrassed to see his reaction, or have to reveal her own. It is over so fast, he is turned inside out, and he can't imagine what his misgivings were before.

He guesses it is losing his virginity, sort of. He is twenty-one years old. For the rest of the trip he walks two feet above the ground and believes that everything leading up to this day can now be forgotten. He owes Basher for this, too.

Falling asleep, cradled next to each other in the tent, under Orion. A thrumming and humming of the night, the occasional snap of dying embers in the fire. He hears the faintest chorus of erratic snoring, far away.

Christiane's high-rise modernist apartment in Montparnasse smells to Harry of summer rain and plans. New money, iron-clad family obligations, an unseemly underworld connection. Harry thinks of the set of a Cary Grant film—*North by Northwest*. When he sits in the living room an art deco lacquer bar reflects the fleshy blob of him and Christiane like a fun house mirror as she fixes him an American cocktail, a sidecar.

    Christiane has a photo of Basher on the mantle; that calm and unsettling glance, resolved and so unlike himself; seeing it so often now, Harry resents it.

    Paris is the bureau's base of operations, but Basher is rarely, if ever, there. He once offered to find Harry a job in the bureau reporting from some third world strike zone, but Harry was not quite ready for that.

    Harry is keeping his affair with Christiane secret. But Basher, in a letter, reveals, *To be honest, Harry, I really didn't think this possible.*

Over drinks, just before he left on a job, Basher gave Harry the once over.

I need to be on the level, here, Basher said. Christiane's got a problem.

Harry took offense, *Well, who doesn't have problems?* He did not thank Basher for the advice.

Basher said, Harry, you can be so conveniently naive.

The second time Harry comes to Paris, before Basher is off to Panama en route to another assignation, Harry makes a point to tell him to fuck off. And mind his own business.

Christiane's world, in Harry's initial simplistic reduction, was an abstraction of camels, bedouins and the Sahara. A terrorist training zone. He knows it's dimensionless, works to bring it to relief, to understand their cultural differences. She talks of her family, making a life in France for so many years, immigrant victories—her cousin makes a fortune importing ornate copper samovars and Kilims from Morocco. They are a secretive family, wary of outsiders, which feeds her intrigue to him. Christiane cringes at his fantasies of the French-Algerian mafia.

Harry empathizes with the immigrant experience, his woman's experience. In these days of wild self-disregard, he considers moving here. He'd have to learn the language. A young man on a journey, he imagines being comfortable in his skin, the unavoidable residue of an international love affair.

The façade of their domestic arrangement makes him feel part of Christiane's life, though she is reluctant to bring him around her friends—they are not his kind of people. The first time he came to Paris, she acknowledged some people at a cafe, but Harry wasn't introduced.

She needs to test him, he is convinced. At her apartment all day, he waits for her to return. He doesn't venture out at first. But the days grow long—he'll have to preoccupy himself. The vaguest idea of what he will do when he returns home is a distant anxiety. In the silence of the evening he listens for the mechanical hum of the elevator driving through the shaft.

Harry studies the abstract paintings in her apartment. One in particular imprints on his psyche, revealing the depths of a singular creative spirit, unhindered: muted and graded colors, toiling swirls of impasto, rectilinear figures on a shallow depth of field. He will never ask her about the obscure artist. The painting becomes an emblem of her life that he is privileged to touch. Christiane quotes her favorite author, Camus, while discussing her father's happy youth in Algiers, that city that *opens to the sky like a mouth or a wound*. She too carries a nostalgia for a life she never knew. Seascapes washed in afternoon thunderstorms, olive and lemon trees cascading down the hills amid ozone and sparkle, bronzed bodies supine on a Mediterranean beach, telemarks from the cliffside vista.

While Christiane attends school, Harry wanders an entire day calibrating and revising his Parisian romance. Paris makes him feel worldly. A transition Basher had already achieved. The city is grimy and hand held, eagerly fondled. The voluptuary can live in Paris and feel at home.

He excavates his rudimentary high school French, hangs out in the cafes where the great expat literary figures have passed through or whiled away hours: Rilke, Beckett, Cortazar. The Left Bank. Walking in the early morning through Montparnasse cemetery, his journal in hand, he offers a nodding tribute to Sartre, buried there two years ago in a royalty worthy spectacle. He perfects the art of making a thimble of bitter coffee last half an afternoon, listening to the babble of a language that he understands nearly every third word of. Watching the reflections in the windows of unfamiliar faces. The purposeful people on the Metro every morning, so many different people in their private struggles.

Regal old buildings in tan and gray clamber high over narrow roadways and as suddenly fade back to reveal vast green parks, iron railings, plane trees, powder sky vistas, the classic view. He cannot get enough, a home he wants to pull around himself like a vast old coat.

In the catacombs the bones of millions of the city's ancient dead are stacked, tunnels veined under the city. Skulls arranged in cruciform. The balled ends of femur joints making a wall plane, set in bizarre geometric order: hearts and circles. He hears of all night parties in the catacombs—doesn't know how to get to them.

Walking along the Seine, the sun pours Autumn space; a river of light, palings on the open path, tree canopies are reflected with double shadows. An aberration of late afternoon sun between two buildings. He sees carts of bones on street corners. This stops him in his tracks. *Seventeen eighty five.* He spends the afternoons in the Luxembourg. At five the gendarme frantically blows his horn calling out in a strangely feminine voice, *Les Jardin est ferme!*

Night after night, waiting for her return, the cool evening settles over Paris and Harry drifts back to Montparnasse to lie awake in Christiane's sea of bed.

School keeps her away far too late. But like religion, she appears in the mists above her bed at three in the morning to make him feel like the most important person in the world. She smells of the cafe and smoky autumn leaves. A willowy silhouette in the dark, she slides naked under the covers. Harry reaches out for her cold limbs. She grips tight to him and curls up fetal. She shivers as he holds her. A hummingbird flitting into consciousness.

She moves in her sleep, cautious under his undiscerning eyes. She moves to get away from him, slippery, under his hands. She demands a return to her element—a world he cannot access. He grapples with her, suspended in a dream. She moves away from him during the conscious hours, and at night, in her sweaty struggle with dreams. What is her life to him, or his to her? An attachment has no logic, makes no sense. He knows he will not escape with clean hands.

He awakes beside her at first light filled with an almost perfect sense of the world. Christiane asleep. Her dreaming, kohl lined eyes, her round face, her long hair cascading before him. Languor at her side. He envies her halcyon sleep and touches her waxy shoulder as if to prove to himself she is real, steps out of bed and wanders to the window. Paris unfurls before him. The sky floats above in a water color veil of clouds over a plain of trembling lights.

Christiane asks Harry to repair a light fixture while she is away at school one day. She says the screwdriver is in a drawer in the kitchen. An excuse, an invitation, to look around. He finds photos and letters. Strangely calligraphed, indecipherable Arabic in a tea and blood colored ink.

He knows they are from a lover, Djembo is the signature, this in English. If Harry isn't blind, the same name as on the painting. Harry digs a little deeper under the leaves and finds lighters, a coil of rubber tubing. A smoke stained spoon. An eye dropper.

In Baja, she had been too elegant and well dressed for their excursion. She was game, as Basher said, with her wide eyes in which

Harry wanted to read her interest. But she walked, away, hours at a time. Came back listlessly.

Each day she carries a shoulder bag, but he never sees a notebook, a sheet of paper. He asks about her studies. Why she never passes through the throngs of students from the Sorbonne, or the University of Paris. He thinks of her unsavory acquaintances—what he comes to think of as a club.

The café, her classroom.

Basher must know them. Harry could have met them in passing, but he isn't sure.

He corners her. He wants to read her determination as playfulness, a desire to appeal to him.

"Can you tell me what it's about?"

She grabs his arm and looks him in the eyes.

"Naive Harry. Now you know how I met Nathan. Why do you think he goes away? He doesn't want you to see who he *really* is."

Hanging around the cafe the next evening, Harry hopes to infiltrate the club. He regrets his initial distance and wariness, too easily heeding Basher's words. Christiane is a woman among men. Harry imagines her their muse, elusive and self-contained.

An outsider among outsiders, he's not the right kind of outsider. They are dark skinned, gilded men in a pantheon to which he will not be admitted. He envies them their entitlement to fulfilled desires. They trade in complexity and ambiguity because they can. Djembo is from Cameroon, Christiane mentioned. This must be the fellow who meets his eyes; he wonders if the guy sleeps with Christiane when Harry isn't around. With a helmet of kinky hair, tattoos.

In a confusion of desire he reads their differences as his weakness. He knows his prejudice is bound to be shallow, a kind of calculus, the *Americano's* impulse of reductio ad absurdum. A register he walks around with because even in Paris he still gets his news from *Newsweek* and the *ABC Evening News with Frank Reynolds*. Christiane's *hermanos* tower over him on the sidewalk, casting a shadow upon a Midwesterner who has come too far afield.

He watches them, surreptitiously, a witness. They are quiet and serious. Like clockwork they stand and leave for—where? A shooting party, as he thinks of it. He imagines them in crumbling, shuttered back rooms, tying off and shooting up.

He doesn't expect to see Christiane. She said she would be in Vincennes.

My luck, he thinks, as Christiane breaks ranks. He reads the riot act in her face, and storms towards Luxembourg Gardens. It's a show. She follows him, calling out.

"Harry. Hold on . . . Do not walk away from me!"

She catches up with him and returns his petulant reprimand. Is she making a case and arguing him from abandoning her?—not that he will. He's come to depend on the evenings she returns to the solid state empty apartment high above Boulevard Raspail. The club never sets foot inside her place that he knows of, she has kept her apartment for the two of them, he thinks, her high palace. She presses the issue.

"Tonight," she says. "Don't wait."

Late in the night he awakes to her pounding on a door. She has locked herself in the bathroom. He gently tells her to unlock the door.

"Harry. But it is stuck!"

She stumbles into the room.

She walks past him, not hiding. "I know how to unlock my goddamned door."

He smells and sees disorder.

Now that it is out in the open, she tries to make light of it. She mocks Harry with a litany.

*You will never understand. You want to know something? I need to do this. That's me. If you accept me, you accept this about me.*

This is my choice. Not everyone gets addicted.

It has nothing to do with *you*.

They are *my* friends.

Aren't we all *dying*, after all?

She comes up behind him. She leans onto his back and holds him. He weakens at her touch. He turns and her body goes limp in his arms. He holds her as she speaks against his arm.

"It is different for me."

They are using her. They do not care about her. Why can't she see that he does?

"This is the way I am. This is me," she says. "I need this."

The language of the fix.

Harry concedes, to separate himself, that he has chosen to come into her world. Truth be told, he blames Basher.

A sense of normalcy, of peace, even, as before he got to know her. The nights in Baja in the tent. Before he could imagine being tethered. He knows he's not getting his fix any other way so he might as well put up with this for a few hours. Look the other way.

Pure torment.

His mind clouds. He does not look. It happens and it isn't

happening. It has nothing to do with you. Christiane appears ghostly in the mists above her bed and makes him feel like the most important person in the world.

To leave now?—out of the question.

He walks in the rain to collect his thoughts and returns late to the apartment. She's not back. His clothes sag and drip. How better to hide morose self-pity.

He stands at her blackened windows dripping a puddle onto the carpet and watches rain sluice down. The rain with the wind sounds like the exterior of the building is wrapped in plastic sheeting. A steady rattle, unrelenting: terminal white noise. He is damned if he will be humiliated into going to look for her.

He forgets to eat the entire day, or could not, and so fries two eggs and desultorily swallows them down.

He lays down on her bed in his damp clothes. He feels as if he is dissolving. Annihilated.

In a dull numbness, somehow he falls asleep. He awakes late to a smell of burning plastic. He finds her curled on her side in the bathtub, her skin cold like a defrosting chicken, blue; her nose wet, her fingers white, her hair damp. Frantic, he shakes her.

Small tremors course through her body.

She awakes with a cough and vomits copiously against the side of the tub, cries out, like a baby. He wipes her face and tries to hide his disgust. The syringe teeters on the tub's edge. Something sharp crackles underfoot and pricks him.

He wraps a towel around her.

She sits up.

"Nathan is dead."

She shuffles to the living room, turns the television on and drops to the floor, switches channels until she finds it. She looks up.

"Last night."

Basher's image, a static passport photograph, sternly stares from the television. A French news voice rings over it.

Harry requests a translation.

"Please. I want to be alone."

In the television over a hotel bar he sees the footage. An affront, a humiliation. Footage he is already burning into memory. He does not want to believe it. The way Basher stands, ready for whatever the assignment demands. A puff of gunfire. On the screen the name N. THOMAS, then the screen shot. The footage, replayed multiple times, slowed down. Basher's French boss, at safe remove from Central America, speaks to the reporter.

Harry hasn't had three good words with Basher in a year.

Harry enters churches, hollowed out mountains of stone, built to last a thousand years, walls thick, impenetrable. He inhales the smoke of burning incense. The language rolls and rises, does not make sense, says one thing. Time ahead and time behind are one and the same. The dying all around him.

He moves through a narrow space and the hollow seeks him out. He becomes lighter than air, lifting into the sky, being blown away. Dust. Ash. Curling. Going through him.

Paris remains wearily glorious. Falling down around him, sinking him into the catacombs.

Basher left too soon.

Christiane stays away for two days.

Harry finds a note. Anger inflames his pride to read *I can no longer do this. Please just forget me and return to America.*

As if she is the key holder to the world.

He returns to the cafe where the club congregates. He does not see her. He stands at the zinc bar and boldly stares them down. He never could imagine wanting to talk to them but will now. They know who he is. Will mock him. This makes it harder.

The fellow he's thought of as the leader, their eyes meet—Harry can see he is being sized up as one of Christiane's *Americano* friends. How many times he sat on the train and heard someone say *Americano*. A derogation. An unbridgeable chasm—they are not friends, they are a club. A club of acquaintances. The acquaintance that comes from an uncomfortable proximity to death, having met in dire straits.

From the sinister sneer on his face, Harry girds himself for an attack. He doesn't know what to say or how to say it.

The French always seem pissed off at him. When he does try, they speak back to him in perfect, yet annoyed, English.

Their talk is loud, as if in excess of themselves. If possible, they are becoming self-conscious in his presence. He can't resist his sudden moment of power.

He forces himself into their circle.

"I think you can help me," Harry says.

Djembo jerks to attention, wary recognition.

"I'm a friend of Christiane's," Harry says, noncommittal. "Harry."

"Problem, Mr. Harry?"

Harry curls his hands into fists so tight that his nails dig into his palms. Djembo smiles and nods. An opportunity. Djembo speaks in a way that Harry thinks it's what he might look like if he was speaking in the dark. Unselfconscious. Wide-eyed in a perpetual fix. Hunted as he thought of all of them. Somehow bored and with a tendency toward self-destruction.

"Oh, I got you," the man says.

"Yes," Harry says, relieved.

"First time's free—for a friend. I can take care of you," he says, holding out his cold hand. "Gem."

Harry doesn't connect the name with the one he'd thought.

"Gem. That's right. A jewel." His English is good. "Meet me outside in half an hour."

Harry walks to the entrance of Luxembourg Gardens and considers walking away, taking the train to Charles de Gaulle and never looking back. But this will only be worse. There is no getting away from it. He doesn't know what to think about what comes next.

He paces the sidewalk, killing minutes. Unawares he bites through his lip and tastes blood. He loiters by a newsstand and scans papers. Basher's picture and a headline:

### Assasinat d'un journaliste reporter Américain rapport des témoins.

Djembo speaks behind him. "Come this way," he says. Harry is hard at his heels. "Don't get ko-zee."

They get into a compact, noisy car for a twenty minute drive into the periphery of the city. Throughout the ride Harry watches Gem. He has problems, no doubt. Harry is reaching a point of no return. He might die tonight. Taking a turn into destruction. Just a matter of time. Looking at him, he flashes on Christiane. Gem makes surreptitious eye contact. He is a grim figure.

Gem parks the car under an overpass and they walk down narrow maze-like streets with cars packed tight against the curb. A quiet residential area, there are few people around. He turns and leads them off the street that becomes a walkway, onto some slippery steps that lead up to a back door of a large Empire style building. More clean and rarified than any he has been in here. A cat slumbering on the window sill kinks its head angrily at their presence.

Gem struggles with a large skeleton key and pushes the door open. Harry tries to speak, to master his unease, but Gem holds up a hand. The familiar smell of Paris, the hot metal and rubber of the subway trains, is thick.

They climb the stairs and enter a room with high, ornate ceilings. An old apartment rigid in its geometry and austerity, unlived in. Sunlight he didn't notice blazes from an interior skylight. The windows are uncurtained and the sun glares on bone white drop cloths scattered on the floor. The smell of the place makes him think of decaying flowers, fraying electrical wires, crumbling facades.

Thoughts of Christiane turn to thoughts of Basher dead, and give Harry a sudden stabbing pain in his chest.

"Here," Gem says, pointing to a green and gold high backed couch covered in plastic. He notices how cold the place is, as if air-conditioned.

"So this is where it happens," Harry says. Gem looks past him.

"What happens?" Gem says, mocking.

"Nothing."

Harry glances around the room. The coiling molding and trim freshly painted. Someone with money keeps the place. Painting ghosts on the white walls. Maybe Christiane's family.

"Does anyone live here?" Harry asks.

Gem sneers at this pretence of familiarity.

"You ask too many questions, man."

Gem goes into the back room through an opening covered by a curtain. What Harry thinks is the kitchen, maybe a pantry. He could run like hell, no one would care.

There are few items. A temporary fold-up card table with paint cans and rollers scattered on top. A dirty washrag. It might have been inhabited at one time, but somehow it seems that it never will be. This could be the club headquarters, if indeed there is one. He did not expect anything comfortable. Not that this was comfortable. Maybe he expected the catacombs.

Gem moves about in the other room. He comes back with a shoe box lid. "This is how we live," Gem says, smiling, as if to make up for his earlier bluntness. Harry sees the needle, feels his blood.

"You like it?"

It is not a question to be answered.

"You want to join us," Gem says.

"I guess," Harry says, to be polite.

"Fucking liar. Harry wants the experience. Fine, Harry. Gem will let you get experienced." Gem sucks on his teeth and looks over Harry's shoulder to the window. "Too bad, 'cause when you start needing Gem's magic, don't come looking for me. I'm going to show you what you're missing, once, then we don't know each other. You got that?"

"Fine," Harry says. "Fine."

"Crazy."

"What?"

"Loco. Amer-e-can-o. Think you can do anything. Like her friend."

"Her friend?"

Gem makes a gun with his hand and holds it to his head and mouths the sound of a shot.

"What do you know?"

Gem gets in Harry's face—he can smell onions on his breath—makes him flinch. Gem whispers.

"Listen, friend—I'll tell you what I know," Gem says. "She Rhiannon. You know that song? *Will you ever win?* She get to you. Cee's got to us all."

Gem laughs to himself.

"I'm teasing! This is a bad way to begin, Mr. Harry. You have to promise we're friends—yes?" Gem says. "Mr. Harry? come on."

"Yes. Friends."

"You don't care. You gonna hurt Gem's feelings." The laugh again.

"What do you want me to say?" Harry says.

"Nothing," Gem says. "From what I can see, you were fucked from day one. I'm the only friend you got right now. You mess with this on your own? You'll be one dead American."

Gem gestures for Harry to roll up his sleeve, which he does.

"Just playing wit' you. Cat and mouse," Gem says. He smiles and shows his teeth, nicotine stained, wide spaced. He ties off the tubing around Harry's arm and tugs. Harry's arm goes numb as he watches.

"Once it happening," Gem says, "you won't remember."

Gem grabs his arm and thumps at it to find a vein.

Before he can see it's happening, the needle is stuck in his arm, his blood mixing with the clear substance, ink in water.

The stick of the needle is dull, not quite painful. Then it feels like a nail. An electrical cord to draw his life from him.

He sees the tube of the needle, a milky ruby cloud, cream in his tea.

His arm grows insensate, he extends his fingers as cold spreads down one side of his body, almost pleasantly, then down the other, and he is sure he is passing out. He is submerged. The shot bolts through him. *Insignificant* echoes from nowhere. He wrenches, tenses, until he can't feel anymore.

Gem speaks, and Harry turns to face him, but he can't understand the words.

He grips the edge of the couch, hanging on. Gravity releases. He rises, floating, filling up with air, expanding beyond the room, lighter than air, insubstantial. Invincible. He will conquer the world. Easy. The pain is gone.

He flies through a tunnel at light speed, blows through walls.

The wake of euphoria.

He doesn't care, he absolutely doesn't care, where he goes.

He can't feel the hollow pit in his stomach, the empty ache, as he tries to remember it. He floats in this absence of himself for a long time—unwilling to move, to not want to shake off the feeling.

*Insignificant.*

He faces Basher, laughing. Basher with glass skin. Basher liquefying, dissolving before him.

He loses it, he falls. He slips the rungs, the grip of the earth, he's in a terrifying free fall, with no chance to take in air, he's suffocating. This is his death, humiliation, he cannot reach out to stop, closing his eyes at the treacherous pass. Falling as fast as he was rising.

He hears a tedious patter of rain. He is drenched in sweat. Freezing and nauseous. His mind is tortured with memories of Basher, gone forever. Christiane. Darkness permeates outside, and the cold. He weakly pulls one of the drop cloths over himself, can't get it on his legs. The odor of linseed oil gives him visions of an undersea cavern, and he struggles through a cough, salivating rancid water. A bright light shines through the window, and the curtains sway into the room. To calm himself he imagines this under his control. He watches the curtain lift and fall, getting hold of himself. Everything is still. The sound of some children outside, or in a room next door. No cars. An aircraft high overhead. He feels a rumble in his stomach and braces himself to get sick. The lovely carpet. Feverish, nausea suspends him in waves, he expects to be sick, but it never comes. Just the horrible weight. He tips into sleep.

He awakes, aware of an unfamiliar place. An empty apartment.

His numb arm frightens him, smacking his knee. He lifts the disembodied arm, rubbery, clammy, with unusual weight, a dummy's arm. A yellow bruise he can't feel.

He comes together, slowly through the hours, as if chunks of his body had been taken out, scrambled, and replaced, and are now settling into a disjointed pattern around his old self, his soul.

The walls are damp, sweating in tropical heat. He remembers arriving there and feels someone's presence. He wants to leave, and quickly, and stands. The blood rushes to his head. He shudders, sickened, to sense what he's done.

The stench, his own body odor, maybe he got sick while asleep. The couch? His self-loathing is unbearable.

He stands, weakly. The left side of his body prickles. The cold through his limbs is overpowering.

A sinister low sky, in magenta and gun metal.

For two hours he wanders, backtracks to find Christiane's apartment.

She has moved everything from the drawer into the cabinet, after his discovery. More prominent, nothing more to hide. His mind is not right. The key is in the drawer. He locks the gear in the cabinet.

He tosses the key down the garbage chute.

He gathers himself, sits on the couch, waiting. He's worn the same clothes for three days running. He leans back and closes his eyes and hopes to sleep, fighting nausea. Agitated. His mouth is dry and yet he doesn't get up for water. He has to stay in one spot, to face her as she enters, to see her fully, on the stage of their demise. He wants her to see him, to acknowledge him. Basher's picture stares ahead. As if he is going to speak out to him from the Cibachrome print about the injustice of premature ends. Damn him.

The nausea, the ache, the grief, overwhelm him. He stands to go to the window but stops himself.

He must stay clear of the windows. He can feel those bare, insubstantial tree limbs. He imagines them all lining the allees reaching up from the black earth to grasp at him. He doesn't dare go to look down to Rue Montparnasse, those arms beckoning him, downward.

He sees their entwined bodies in free fall, smacking onto the gum dappled pavement. The thought is sickening. The branches won't catch them, won't break a fall, they will slip right through, stones into the soft earth.

With each vibrating pass of the elevator, he sees her walking in. He closes his eyes to see her, entering the building, in a rush it reverses itself, he sees her crumpled up on the ground. He had crossed over, violated the rules. He could hear the elevator slide and the metal door unlatch, her steps, the door flings open in fury.

She stands in the doorway rigid for battle.

"What the fuck Harry."

Christiane goes for the drawer where she used to keep her gear. She pulls the drawer out and the contents cascade onto the tile. The photos. The letters.

"Had enough?," she says.

Harry's mesmerized, amused with himself, a survivor.

"Where is it. Where is my bag?"

She yanks other drawers open and slams them looking for the key.

He gestures to the garbage chute.

"You fucking go down and find it," she howls, whacking the cabinet. "Go now!"

She pulls a hammer from the drawer and swings it at him. He knocks it out of her hands. She swings her fists fast at him. He resists.

She grabs Basher's picture, clutches it to her chest and falls to the floor, heaped upon herself, crying. He watches, miserable, distant.

Christiane would often say, *We were never worthy. We shared something special.* We: Christiane and Basher.

She picks up the hammer and runs at the cabinet.

No one plans for the end. Like there can be no end.

"Fuck you. Get out. Of my house."

Christiane puts a chair behind the cabinet and torques it from the wall. Briefly, poised in still space at gravity's urging, it leans face forward. In the moment of silence, an eternity, between heaven and hell, it slams to the floor with a crush of glass and shattering wood.

# IV. AMALGAM

Easy going, slow going, he must have thought, knowing the aspects of that particular gun, popular model, AK, the boy waving the barrel overhead. Dwarfing the child of the forest his friend made an appeal to, now facing him down ninety feet. Let's trade camera for gun, shall we. A camera versus a gun? he might have thought, hardly a fair trade off, if he could have managed it, but safer. In that tension that was his job's daily uncertainty, the laughter at the last moment seemed to the child like a taunt, a cry of challenge: prove yourself. A child who did not understand that he was playing into the hands of some larger, indefinite agent. He'd wanted to help, he'd loved that place and its sloe eyed children. Did not want this injustice. A tragedy a country's going to seed, falling apart like that. The road a narrow path to paradise, he was there to show them. One shot, a spray of bullets, the number makes for uncanny accuracy, to the chest, to the heart. Just an accident, he wanted to believe for a split second.

LAX is unusually quiet for a Monday afternoon. He'd have to be in Cancun by seven that night, for the shuttle flight arranged by the company that ran the tours at Rancho Nacon. He'd printed out the twelve pages of boiler plate about the resort that he had to request via e-mail. He insisted to Janelle as she packed his bag that it was not a pleasure trip. "Should I pack a suit? Aren't you going to swim?" she'd asked.

From Mexico, it will be on to Guatemala and the attempt to find the village where Basher last set foot. He believes Rancho Nacon to be the last place Basher ventured from before that trip to the village.

Janelle offered a suggestion. "Take your prescription."

Harry left without calling Janelle (she went to work early) and in the glassed in, oddly dim, nearly empty corridors of polished tan terrazzo, he wandered with only a small army shoulder bag, looking for a pay phone. No checked baggage—he had a feeling it was going to be hard to keep tabs on, to lug around.

Grey is the color of anonymity, he thinks, as he presses his forehead to the glass and watches, waits. Outside, stillness, random and sudden motions and muffled sounds. Distant flags lilt in the breeze. Fields of concrete. The swift movement of heavy planes through warm space.

Two Asian boys press their hands and noses to the glass beside him, to feel the rumble of the triple insulated pane.

The ever long moment for the tail, standing in view from behind a hangar, moving slowly forward and in full view of the wall of glass, lifting, the roar, the strain, the heave into space, the point of no return. A ponderous plane, like a bloated bird, loaded down. The thin wings give the illusion that they are bouncing like planks over the shimmering tarmac as the plane rolls.

East above the horizon, the planes grow in immensity, until they drop low and disappear behind the hangar canopy, coming into view in the window before him as the reverse thrust spreads into the air.

Out over the ocean, toward the western horizon, they become specular in the rays of the sun, curls of heat glinting, silhouetting, rendering them into dark points in the distance, indistinguishable, soon, invisible. They hang, to appear almost unmoving, heat trails at the limits of the city, over improbable chasms of time.

He figures this will be the last phone call. For awhile. Shoulder bag heavy.

In a rhomboid of sunlight.

"Janelle Gilmartin, please. Thanks."

Cars link swiftly through a gap, behind a railing, beneath the overpass. An aircraft rattles the glazing, the air is burst. The sound fading into a rustle. An orange 737 stops on the tarmac, awaits departure. A ghostly white plane moans in ascent over the blue ocean.

Resigned. He hears it in an overheard conversation while he thinks it. A woman and a chattering man who resembles his Ethiopian neighbor. She works for the security detail, is patient. They sit in a corner, coding the background of Harry's distracted thoughts. He tries to discern the mood.

"This is what I'm saying," he hears himself rehearse—or only thinks it—"I can't tell you what I will find until I go away and find it."

Returning from Michigan, drifting in the tubular belly of one of those behemoths, he recalled seeing HOLLYWOOD on the swatch of brown green hill so familiar, an itinerant homeland for all the time he's spent here.

"One week. Max."

Walking from one terminal end to the next is a microcosm of driving across Los Angeles, it can take hours. Standing at windows and feeling the seed of energy in the pit of his stomach, the knowledge of an escape, or, rather, the obverse, having made it into a trap. If he does not let the failures that have gotten him to where he is stop him, if he does not seek to gain from his friend's death, he can look at this journey as an immense reckoning.

## Excerpts of letter from Basher to Harry, postmarked San Juan del Sur, Nicaragua. January 31, 1981

```
—The light down here is--different. You'll know what I
mean—
```

Over the blue sheet of the gulf, morning sunlight mirrors blinding patches through the clouds. Who knows the depths of—your suffering—no, that's too easy. The depths of your thought, your project, your higher purpose. Who cares, seems more like it.

Harry meant to recover his relationship with Basher, even two decades late, and put it to rest. He had stopped trying to re-imagine Basher. The recognition that the memories were there, and had been, no matter what came later.

He came down here with Janelle at a time when he thought he might give up *Deconstructing Nathan Thomas*. But he had not thrown everything in a bundle and left it behind. Basher's letters kept drawing him down to the equator (near there, Costa Rica, similarly), years later. Something in the humid equatorial air inspired him.

Hastily, he gathered up this journal labeled, in a moment of past idealism, *ephemera*—a fancy, really—and carried it with him. The initial reflections on a Basher screenplay. When he had been fixated on ephemera, and his idealism grew wings.

. . . Sunlight streams into the window, too bright. An all seeing eye: in that eye I am all seen, all known. The world suffused with light, the wash of amber. They flew over islands and aimless topography, miles high, blue light, a cloud map below, seasonless days. That light like grace.

An afternoon suddenly cold, covered in clouds and drenching thunderstorms. The entirety of his trip was to recollect the light. An homage to his friend? He took to describing the sky, the light, the water, the reflections on the water at five in the afternoon. This is all he wrote. He has only to consult this journal that he will lose in time; its thick water stained pages rippling and curling, like the diagram of a wave. Not so long ago. Page 56. Trying to describe the light, the color, the way his friend might have seen it:

*We walked tonight down a curving dirt road into the words;* typo *intermittent huts and houses at the edge of the sea, the rain a constant threat . . .*

Harry took photos. Janelle with sunset. Stormclouds.

*Clouds roll in each afternoon, a phosphorescent blue with edges of orange of the hidden setting sun. Large bright palm plants rocking in the breeze. The distant beat of an open bar playing techno music. The chitter of insects sequestered in the deep folds of exuberant foliage. With the wind, and the ocean, an unrelenting shuss of white. Layers of sound, when the color fades into shadow green, into blank night . . .*

```
—The light gives me a lot to work with. And space.
I have the space to compose with.—
```

Remember the lotus-eaters. The cabana came back to him. The yellow bug light filled out and suffused the room with a mellow tint. Janelle mentioned them. *This is the domain of the lotus-eaters.* Harry wrote down, *demesne*. Surfer dudes and gals stayed there for months at a time in the bathwater surf, cruising the endless unpopulated beaches. He took crazy dives into ten foot waves, had an unpleasant drink of the salty ocean. They return to the hut and shower under cool water. Falling asleep with the heat on their skin, waking in the sun dappled shade of a palm. The clouds are pulled over in the afternoon, like curtains.

You want to be like them, she said.

Harry denied his lotus status while looking at flowers in the sand. *Demesne. The word means domain, estate. (Pronounced like 'domain'.)*

They stopped to buy ice cream at Dos Pinos. Or that would be, *the* Dos Pinos.

The locals gathered here each night to collect around the open bar under the fluorescent light. *Doble cicolleto,* Harry said, surprising himself because the counter man had understood him. The man pointed to the group behind him. Warily, Harry and Janelle looked. One of the fellows grasped a terrified owl wrapped in a claw snagged, bloodied t-shirt. Its black eyes bulging. Harry thought they expected him to be impressed by this spectacle, but it annoyed him, and he feigned amusement. Surprised at his disgust.

At the outdoor cafe, another expatriate Austrian (she told them) trying to find herself among the lotus eaters, served them in a periwinkle bikini. He wasn't far from self-conscious indiscretion—prompted, an animal—she cast her diabolic eyes like two quick laser points, setting him up for the kill. Stacking the deck again. Sheer fantasy, intoxication, prey as ever to curiosity. Her fragrant perfume left a muffled trace on the rim of his lechero. He liked when women sought his attention, as if he would not have noticed them otherwise.

Janelle, acknowledging the woman, the other, shut Harry out and went for a run. Harry sat on the beach. Janelle needed a way of controlling him when she felt him to be out of her control. How Harry had taken control of her life had been her frustration. He might say the same of her.

```
—You can have an entire beach to yourself—
```

A desert, the boiling ocean, the wind blowing all away, an edge: this is what the planet will look like when every last trace of civilization is gone.

*A wave will appear with aquamarine blue that turns to white foam, a pure virginal white.* What a redundant phrase. *In other places the water appears brown, muddy, or mossy. (The waves. The cresting part of the wave, does it have a name? An apex, perhaps. Note: look up wave mechanics. There must be such a thing. Fluid dynamics?) The reflector* awkward, because he didn't know what else to call it *is the apron, where the water washes onto the beach, reflecting the powder of the sky. The apron is the reflector. The curvature of the earth seems obvious, self-evident. There is a curve at the edge of the disc . . .* That vantage point made him think of Robert Irwin's "Scrim veil—Black

Rectangle—Natural light".

How difficult to describe colors, especially when the colors are so varied within a range: blue, green, etcetera. Does one describe them with other colors? This blue is the blue red would be, if red were blue.

Montezuma: The water, depending on the angle of incidence of the sun's rays, looks darker here. At this hour, five p.m., the water is a deep blue, with small shadows on the otherwise mirror-like rippling surface.

Three days in Montezuma.

*Lots of dense, shiny hardwood floors and paneling. A forties feeling wood deck with wicker chairs and rockers, gnarled tree trunk posts and fish net railings. One thinks of Hemingway's Key West. Or that essay by E. B. White about the Keys. This is the way keys form. That side of the peninsula resembled more what Harry had seen of Italian seaside towns, a la Capri, which then made him think of Antonioni's La Aventurra and Il Deserto Rosso. They sat on the deck while he took these selfsame notes.*

```
—I took a private boat. You can hire one at the docks—
```

*Ferry to Puntarenas. A ferry of Central American color and character, sitting full in the water like a torpid albatross. The bay here is like the Mississippi, with the stifling humidity. We move off effortlessly, no bumps, no rocking. The boat rumbles, so heavy, gravitating through the water. The surrounding hills grow hazy in the distance—they protrude from the water, forested with green. A bowl bodied pelican, wingtips tapping the water, beak thrust horizontal, lazily arcing ahead of the ferry. A warm gust of exhaust settles on the deck. This is one of those places that, unless you come here, you don't quite realize it exists. If someone pointed it out on the map you wouldn't be sure what is there. A body of water, but what on the horizon?. . .*

From there the silent treatment taxi ride, in a red Range Rover, for almost an entire morning, to another destination. A sudden rain had expelled the humidity and washed the dust from the streets. Sun cleaned they stepped into the fragrant air, a hint of sulphur and orchids, like entering a new world, riven of old concerns, an impending understanding, periwinkle long forgotten. They disembarked like they were on a blind date, at the concrete and slick marble, sharp angles and hard geometry of some developer's notion of a resort on the sloping Switzerland of Mt. Arenal. Sod like carpet out their back door. The vegetation terminally lush from the downpours, daily—the evening skies are afire. They sat and played gin rummy under cover of the stucco porch while suicidal moths the size of small birds jagged and angled for the porch light.

The rain steamed on the lava flows that washed down the side of the volcano. At night Harry lay in bed and kept the curtain parted so he could watch the bright lava rolling in what looked like slow motion, dusting the mountainside. Balls of molten rock dropping off dispersing a gray swath through the forest. Grinding and rumbling out of time with the visual, like some far off event. They ask their guide, "How far away is it? Is it safe?" and yet do not get a straight answer. He was quite certain the catastrophic event—though possible at any moment—would not happen while they were there. The girl from the town said, "I don't think about it," laughing. He watched the mountain purling a stream of grey residue into a ceiling of immense cumulonimbus clouds.

So hot some days, steamy, even. Yet they opted for mud baths on that day it rained hard and the temperature dropped twenty degrees. The mud cold and clammy.

Harry took the serpentine kid's slide and nearly beaned himself out of commission. He shuddered with acknowledgement, the possible triumphant splash of blood and humor, the thought of his twitching body sinking to the bottom of the kiddie pool. Floating to a stillness and certain death. An inelegant exit unworthy of his friend's memory. Janelle, waiting with a sweating margarita poolside, at first demonstrative—quicker than he could say, I'm sorry—critical.

```
—I had a few run-ins. Scary rides. Nothing to bother
about. I'm still here—
```

A seat gripping tear in a taxi across the wet roads. Are we in a hurry? Janelle asked. Off to the tourist paradise or nightmare—from their lodgings—to the more swank, at least in its unapologetic presentation, resort. Japanese walkways and mahogany bridges through cascading foliage, stopping points, cloistered benches and canopied bars, away from the European, American and Asian throngs that have gathered there—outrageous prices at two or three times what they were accustomed to, and a ridiculous entrance fee. Soaking in the pools, he waited while Janelle got a massage. Sulfurous water poured in grey rivulets into the slimy rock bottomed pools. At the end, all degrees of ill will forgotten, a surrender to the warm water.

An ion charge of sea washed air and tropical humidity is noticeable. The small plane skims in close enough to discern the modern buildings, pale green reefs submerged in shallow aquamarine tide pools, the bone pale concrete infrastructure and sparkled finger of an island. The plane tucks into a sharp bank, turning toward the mainland over a vast forest where snaking new roadways are being carved out in long, narrow swaths. At the end of these unfinished paths, yellow mechanical implements sit, toys in a child's abandoned sandbox, progress through the tangle, one foot at a time. Projecting above the tree canopies electrical towers hang through the fastness linked by bowing wires. Harry recalled pictures of the peninsula taken inland—the vista reminded him of certain parts of Michigan—and, gauging from the bushy skein in the airplane window, as the reality set in, he is duly impressed by the flat green expanse.

He watched the sunlight portholes, cast upon the curves of the plane's interior, making their way down and across the seats. He liked to imagine himself in the geography, his presence within the landscape—

where he'd be soon enough. He'd looked over topographical maps of Guatemala, and the Yucatan, of its peninsular aspect, in this way it was like Michigan, except tropical. He didn't doubt that for all of the fascination with such a new and essentially exotic place, if he spent enough time here he could make it seem as dull as Michigan was to him now. This is what it was to know a geography intimately.

They flew further onward toward a private landing strip. What he knows of the host, Ferdinand Malatesta, and the estate tucked away into the depths, is a haze of uncertainty as they draw upon the landing strip.

Harry would stay on the level, not think of the cross purposes of his goals. Stepping onto the tarmac he is hit by a gust of heat and, as he catches a glimpse of the rain washed macadam, he regrets the words, or lack of them, he last had with Basher.

It had been 68 degrees that morning in Los Angeles, now stomach-achingly far away.

Harry had found information on Rancho Nacon through the internet and emailed, making contact with a woman named Mayor.

Rancho Nacon provided adventure escapes on 50 acres of pristine, undeveloped land. The management's goal was to provide a foundation for the promotion of indigenous culture. Malatesta hoped to open his doors to an artistic community, creating a setting with hints of utopian gloss.[1] Harry tracked down the community from Basher's correspondence.

---

1  The CV in Rancho Nacon's introduction packet had a brief and vague footnote on Malatesta's background, what Harry guessed was a clandestine military involvement with two previous presidential administrations, the years of which pointed to Reagan's and, briefly, Bush senior's, before Malatesta presumably headed off into the brush to retire to Rancho Nacon. Harry would work a way around to his subject of interest.

When he explained his situation to Mayor, including providing a release and indemnity disclosure, she advised him to book his tour through the normal channels, if he wanted to get any real access. This helpful correspondent further advised him to downplay his media affiliation (a tenuous connection, at best).

What he'd contrived to provide for *Munificence* is a dutiful five thousand word profile of Raleigh Dawes, a resident artist who had developed a passion for the lost civilization of the Maya. The greater goal was to acquire some detail of local color for the documentary and weave in the larger picture of Basher's unexplored, expatriate, life.

Rancho Nacon might have a life on the page. Words catching fire, or sizzling out into a dwindling smoke trail. What had brought Basher down here?

Harry had gotten a reservation for the mid-week bargain, selecting an option from the "Espionage Incognito," "Mayan Discovery," and "Caribbean Sunset" packages. The "Espionage Incognito" was recommended for daring single persons; "Caribbean Sunset" was a romantic escape for couples. "Basic" was another option, sans drama, for the timid.

"Espionage Incognito" delivers him in a veil of secrecy, blindfolded, in keeping with the allure. This meant a terrifying drive at speeds unaccountable, where he briefly lifted his blindfold to a blur of oncoming traffic. This was met with a disapproving reprimand ("No senior"). With the precise location of Rancho Nacon, within range of state protected land and, as the website claimed, "literally thousands of undiscovered Mayan temples," they were keen to remain unknown to the outside world. Malatesta was selling cabana plots within a short walk from the Caribbean for an initial investment of 17,000 dollars

American—after an exhaustive background check, of course. This was the newest development at Rancho Nacon, promoted as a re-imagining of Club Med for a more unconventional, less desirous of materialistic trappings, bohemian clientele. The cloister of mystery about its exact location was possibly a gambit to heighten an anti-establishment appeal. If the prospective client was interested, they would be given more information and, presumably, actual directions to a selection of available plots with upgrade options.

There are a number of out buildings for the guests. Harry is the last guest to arrive and the place is only half full, still, getting put up in an insect spray ridden cabana at the far reaches of the grounds.

The full layout of the compound had yet to be explored. Harry assumes he has free reign in the main building, the most public of the spaces, a wide concrete villa abutting the beach and reaching back into the jungle-like grounds. The owner had taken inspiration from local lore, installing a kind of neo-Mayan hierarchy, in plan, and in detail, on the architecture: corbel arches and faux stone relief of jaguars and warriors, polychromed for authenticity. The walls are unnecessarily thick, with a kind of Mayan construction in their exaggerated vertical sloping, in a desire to provide a fortress against the hurricanes that come every season. Retractable wood slat screens can be attached to barricade all the exterior openings.

Harry has been indirectly jotting notes on the place, reminding himself to choose words carefully, avoiding mention of Basher. With the cursory reading he has done about the Maya and the ancient practice of ritual sacrifice, he cannot escape the bloody reference as he squints into the distance. The natural beauty of the place forces him to consider a phrase he jotted into his notes: *the re-birth in amber light*.

In his beach slumber, Harry imagines the flood waters rise like a backed up sewer and send every unmoored object in a purge through the grounds, across the rutted dirt roads that become like channels, until every last manmade thing is left in tatters. The wide tiled floors can be washed clean of this detritus, the dead fronds and skeletal branches, the sea wrack Harry stepped through on that morning's walk along the beach: a child's shoe, a gigantic wooden cable spool, plastic containers of various sizes, colors and shapes, with paper labels long effaced, wooden posts from some washed out dock, an orange construction pylon, mangled soccer balls, the disposable by-products of a material culture out of control. He sees in all this carelessness a society that, with a surfeit of natural beauty, has inevitably disregarded aesthetic housekeeping.

Opening his eyes after falling asleep under the damp tree canopy, he is blinded by the walls drenched in a blaze of equatorial sunshine.

Intrigued by one of the guests, a woman in his periphery. To watch the guests at their leisure makes him feel he is living vicariously, somehow. Imagined hands, imagined touches. With the gulp of water he takes one of the pain pills, watches her. But no time for such distractions.

Rancho Nacon's link to Basher's life is a vast curiosity, and what he learned now might add significant layers to *Deconstructing Nathan Thomas*. He notes:

*If anyone delves into another person's life — even someone they think they know — they will likely discover so many things that they didn't know. Many things they might not want to know.*

A voice across the sand calls to him.

"A new guest. You must see the cenote!"

Malatesta?

Harry is on the tour of the grounds, with Zagros leading the way, Malatesta's custodian.

Zagros whangs away at ropes of vine.

"There are thousands, literally thousands of undiscovered cenotes, just like this one," Zagros says. Just like the hundreds of Mayan ruins buried under the centuries of brush, one has only to look for them. Progress is slow going, the Mayan preservation council is eager to reclaim these sites and prettify them for tourism.

After a fifteen minute slog through the bramble they arrive on a small plateau. Zagros walks the perimeter to find the opening, a hole in the ground, and leads the way with a flashlight. "Welcome," he says, "to the mother of all cenotes."[2]

---

[2] Cenote (*pronounced*: si-'nO-tE. In Maya, this means 'sacred water'), are underground stalactite and stalagmite filled caverns of fresh water, unique to the geography of the Yucatan peninsula. These were most likely formed in the aftermath of an asteroid, sixty-five million years ago. The Mayan civilization, which thrived for five centuries during the late Roman Empire, considered these cenotes sacred portals into the spirit world, and the bed chamber of their feared sun god, Kinich Ahau (also known in Maya as *Ah Xoc Kin*).

The Chicxulub crater, so called because it is centered on the town of Chicxulub on the edge of the Yucatan peninsula, and the asteroid that begat it, were largely speculative, until evidence from oil geologists in the early 1980s identified disparities in gravitational fields at the Yucatan coast. Further geological exploration yielded evidence of a major catastrophic asteroid impact with milennia-long consequences.

At the end of the Cretaceous era, when the Pangean continent devolved into the land masses of Laurasia and Gondwanaland and giant mastodons walked the earth, an asteroid the size of Manhattan slammed into the Yucatan peninsula. The catastrophic impact and blast created a firestorm and earth-wide cataclysms, turning this limestone shelf into liquid and releasing millions of tons of sulfur and carbon into the air and rendering the oceans a sulfurous toxic stew. The resulting atmosphere blocked the sun leading to a planetary winter of massive devastation that is believed to have killed off most of the dinosaurs. This event is known as the Cretaceous-Tertiary Extinction.

After millions of years, the degrading of limestone layers over the breccia at the rim of this crater allowed the formation of the myriad cenotes. When the sea level dropped during the last ice age, the water that filled these caverns washed out and the shelf of the Yucatan resurfaced. In an effect known as halocline, the freshwater, rather than mixing with the sea water, remained on top of it.

In 2000, the space shuttle Endeavor and the Shuttle Radar Topography Mission set

They crawl through the small opening, squeezing in, ducking down and stepping with caution onto an almost hidden ladder attached to the ground. A dozen steps down is a platform. The interior is dark but for a light well that angles dim mid-day sunshine rods across the rough walls and flickers with the plashing of water lapping against the rocks. The floor has been carefully shimmed and fitted with long planks to make a stable platform. Harry stands at the edge waiting for his eyes to adjust. He begins to make out forms, shafts of light beaming into the pearly, opalescent water.

"The Maya feared water," Zagros informs him.

One fever plagued night that week Harry would awake sweating on his bed in the vast cabana to the silence, a silence like death, a tomb, from a dream he recalled in which he had imagined himself trapped in a kind of wine cellar storage room that was deep as this cenote in the ground, while a rising level of warm water slowly subsumed him. In the claustral dark water he saw beams of light and imagined trapped divers. He awoke and wrote down:

*Does one imagine in a dream? Isn't dream more like reality; does the realm of imagination "evince its state" and become rather the present reality?*

about mapping the surface of the Earth on a large scale. Endeavor, making 16 daily orbits of the Earth on an 11 day mission (176 orbits), angled belly up, tail forward at 17,000 miles per hour, or 4.7 miles per second (it would cross Manhattan lengthwise in 2.76 seconds) gathered interferometry data using outboard payload radar and tracking and navigation antennas on a 200 foot mast. This use of two sources for data gathering, at the Shuttle's body, and at the extended mast, yielded more accurate data readings than had been achieved on previous sorties. Topographic elevation models of the Yucatan were then computer modeled from this data using shading and color coding in which the 3 mile wide edge of the Chicxulub crater is rendered as a dark green. Geographically, the lower half of this impact crater encompasses an area nearly perfectly defined by the bottom half of a circle, from the town of El Renate on the North, arcing radially across the Yucatan plain through Merida and on the West at Celestun. At the edge and vicinity of this crater are where the many thousands of subterranean cenotes lie.

He stared at the cool walls of the hall that night, perpetually damp; at least, this is what he saw and imagined, it is likely a glossy paint he had avoided getting close enough to investigate.

Their world, the Maya, what they didn't know, was unaccountable strangeness, they could never part with their abeyance to the earth gods, the unknown, the supernatural. To suggest they were not enlightened, however, is to question if we are, for that matter. Knowledge being relative to its time in history.

Exhilaration, free-floating, as he hits the water. Resolve falls away in that moment the grip of the cold water surrounds his fragile flesh.

Harry turned to go under, trying to forget the surroundings, Rancho Nacon, and the immensity of Zagros, who throws him fins.

"You'll appreciate an exploration," Zagros says. After which he gingerly tosses the face mask. "Don't drown," he calls out.

Harry swims, going down into crooked chasms. His eyes adjust. In the darkness, small beams of light create bold laser-like shafts that iridesce on the rocky edges of walls. Light bursts through, a flood lamp. Green and yellow stalactites drip down, stone icicles, impeding his passing through a cavern. Below the water, he goes toward the light, further from the echoing voice—still in his head—of Zagros.

It's been awhile since he's felt so invigorated—almost a primal sensation, the water.

As if going away all is forgotten. He'd never completely feel he could appease Janelle. She must be glad for this break. She would have had him give this work up, though she would never come out and say so. Still. He might not have begun *Deconstructing Nathan Thomas* except while with Janelle. This one will go into production, will see the big screen, at least Telluride, of this Harry is determined. Find the place where Basher died. Do a few interviews. Cull this research. Actually sit down . . . write the goddamned documentary.

Apropos Yucatan and points south he claimed a paycheck from *Munificence* and the Raleigh Dawes profile. Janelle had carefully packed a suitcase which he further stripped down to essentials: a list of contact information, the remainder of the oxycodone prescription, some of the documents from Basher's boxes, and, so as not to forget Janelle, a picture of the two of them on their Costa Rica vacation a year ago, the one of them waiting for the boat that would take them to the reef.

In the photo, in a bikini, Janelle shows off her tattoos. She had once told him they were from her youth, and silly, but she still liked them anyway. They were scars of a dysfunctional adolescence, she said. She called them a work in progress. He saw the maintenance of a facade. Her tattooist, failing to obliterate a name from that youth inscribed on her hip, and Janelle wishing to be rid of the tag's mnemonic, blotched a mass of dark ink there. He expected a line of text blacked out as if on a classified document, saw instead a crushed caterpillar.

On a boat from Montezuma, they were taken far out to some prime snorkeling reef, shallow but far from shore. Janelle became still and unnerved as they held tight onto the gunwales as the boat slammed the bucking waves. To their left, along the shore, the water dropped away from them in breaking waves, a steep precipice above the beach. Her weakness humbled him. She was usually so bold. He reached out to comfort her but in her anger and dismay—as much at herself as at him, he considered—she ignored him, and could only look at the deck of the boat.

The reef with dense grass-like bundles and mossy blades waved in the heaving clear Pacific. They floated in the water for over an hour and he imagined his skin turning luminescent, textured, as if staying so long in the salt water it might slough off, becoming one with the ocean. The boat was far away, Janelle worried they would be left out there, and Harry kept trying to draw her further out. A kind of challenge. The white prow piercing the horizon line, he couldn't get far enough away, defiant that the turbulent motion of the water would not defeat him.

When Janelle was nauseous, Harry was trying to get back to her, too distant to do anything. He saw her pausing with her head above the surface, the space and light between them turning her blue, as she writhed and got sick in the waves.

Then as now, he felt at one with the fish who swam along unaware he was not one of their kind, until they sensed his immense form blocking their sun on the sand floor. He would trail this lumbering bull of a fish with its tentacled face and bulging eyes, noticing its increasing panic as his shadow passed overhead. Silvery edged fish came obliviously in packed clouds through his outstretched hands, slipping between his fingers.

The water pulled them along, unfastened objects suspended in the jelly of the earth. A life in the womb.

What divides us from the real and the not real? This underwater world was a reality he did not know. He felt the cool strands of a woman's hair stroking his cheek, sea grass. Whipping his face. He thinks he might be dreaming this, or imagining it. Hallucinating. How does he know it is a woman, he just does. He sees it colored henna it's called, which was not Janelle.

He had to get away.

Or go forward, toward another passage further down that appeared to lead to the light outside. He starts to resurface, with barely the room to get his head up for air. He keeps his head under and blows water out through the snorkel. The voice gone. A memory, a bit of a disturbance.

*How the old anxieties are replaced by the new.*

Standing at his Gram's looking out or looking in. Blue shadows at four p.m. in snowbanked hills. Winter flies drop from the window head, dying their slumberous winter deaths. Cobwebs drift in slow drafts. Lady bugs snap onto the sill, the walking wounded, trailing their amber wings, lacking the energy to fly. The gypsy moth nostalgizes its terrestrial chains, slow purling and surrendering its milky eyes to the void while evading four legged beings covered in fur or slime, like himself. Rebirth, metamorphosis. Outside looking in, or upside looking down, through the looking glass, beneath the surface. Standing in the blue field of snow while the flakes pile around. An anemone world, unobservant, unselfconscious. Darting slippery beams of flesh. The horizon surrenders the opaque universe. Light through air, heat through air bending, refracting, sourceless.

Nausea writhes his body and transmogrifies his tumescent cadaver hands into vast, unfolding wings. Like the moth whose paper wings' powder rubbed off against his black t-shirt when he caught it in a futile dance in the confusion of moon shadow and Gram's porch light. *That will kill him*, Gram said, *that's a protective layer*. By the time it is discovered on the creature's wings, it is too late.

Now that you have your wings, you won't be long for this world.

He emerges, unfolding from the sacral energy in his coccyx, the latent wings an archaic twist on sentience. In his neophyte state he forgets what his years had conditioned him to become.

Flashes of light. Heat flows quickly. Combustion is spontaneous, carbon and water, ultimately, riding out ahead of the fireball, charring in its flaring and evanescence even as it trades on that initial promise. Because he can fly he goes out just enough ahead, very confused now, his wings sizzling like Chinese paper lanterns that usually bring enlightening through them, casting evolutionary doubt into this whole primoridial mess. Was he not just underwater, while at the same time recognizing that his change of state has just upset the whole anthropo-cosmic stew?

Rise.

Eyes upturned to be in motion, floating to the sky. Going toward the light, toward the light. To surface, a pressure sucking gasp, one still long for this world. Tattered wings a dream like fish food in the sea balm, spreading around. Sunlight, warmth.

Harry gasps for air.

In the dim light someone much smaller than Zagros stands at the edge of the steps.

"He sent me to get you," she says, reaching out her hand as if to pull him out.

The first impression, before you know who the person is, has an unparalleled effect on the memory.

He recognizes her from the beach.

"May I ask a question," Harry says. "Don't you work for Malatesta?"

"Don't be ridiculous."

Mayor.

"Do we know each other?"

He shouldn't have taken those painkillers before hitting the water.

Malatesta it must be, standing in the doorway. Ferdinand "Frank" Malatesta. Shrouded in the light he holds a match to his Cohiba, the sputtering flame flashing on his ruddy face. It flickers and glances off his glasses, the kind that look sliced off on top. Thin and slight, with a deflated soccer ball paunch, he was an inversion of a drug lord. His ludicrous Pappillon, basking in his shadow, waits for attention with an eager, maniacal skittishness. Its ruffled fur back floats in the air like freshly fluffed laundry.

Malatesta squares Harry up.

"I see you've met my provocateur, the unflappable Mayor. Are you sure we haven't met—Harry . . . Ogletree? I think I would have remembered. You have seen Raleigh? Furtive trimmer of trees."

Harry had noticed an unusual looking caucasian man working with a rake and a giant pair of clippers on the fringes of the estate who did not look up from his work.

Malatesta smiles.

"Unfortunately, he's been called away for some business. Maybe I can enlighten you."

"Okay."

"You will see for yourself," Malatesta says, squatting down to pet his dog. "I'm not going to lie about the center's progress. This one's been perfecting his practical skills."

Harry settles in for the show. This is a good opportunity to perfect his listening skills.

"Oh, I'm sorry," Malatesta says. "He's—Raleigh—he is our resident artist."

"I gathered that."

"He's a detail man. He helped design a large part of this," Malatesta says, outstretching his hands. "The center. He has a healthy fascination with the Maya. His work should be more well known. He did some art house films a few years back, quite successful." His intonation suggests doubt.

"Some of us here, we've burned our bridges the way a cat has lives. I think Raleigh's on his seventh or eighth. His art is more important to him than the acquiring of money, since you might wonder about it. But does art have any affect on this world anymore? If you make that your purpose. You are a writer—correct?"

Malatesta doesn't wait for Harry to respond.

"Raleigh might have bought his way into the art world at another time, but he wants to do it on a legitimate level. His film foray was curious. He was, almost by principle, aiming for obscurity. Raleigh offers an analogue, of course, to my project here . . . That magazine, they didn't send you down here to secretly write about me, now, did they?"

"They didn't send me," Harry says carefully. "I solicited them.

Raleigh Dawes intrigues me."

Harry tries to keep to himself, wanting to disguise his ulterior motives. He could care less about Raleigh Dawes. He believes, for the briefest moment, that he will have to fake interest. Curious by default. He might come right out and ask about Basher.

"I'll tell you what I'm intrigued by," Malatesta said suddenly. "My book. Can I tell you about that?"

"Please."

"You can't really believe what you might hear.

"I'll give you what you came down here for. I think. You'll get a boring story about an ex-military man who is trying to live quietly, maybe even make a change in the world. With Raleigh, you will get the—what is the word?—the analogue. This I can tell you about. I can't tell you so much about myself, without sounding pompous. Every man loves to hear his own voice, Harry, and I'm no different. And you certainly aren't going to get an accurate picture from any of these folks. But I'll be honest with you. None of them trust themselves around me. They are afraid of me, I think. They have no reason to be. But let me tell you about Raleigh."

Since he had to be thinking of producing the actual piece, this Raleigh figure could be an interesting subtextual element to the story. The team would then have to send a videographer down, which was unlikely, considering the byzantine secrecy with which they had delivered him here. Harry would rally his descriptive abilities.

"This is all covered in my book," Malatesta says. "I can see, now you're interested."

Harry nodded. It was easier this way. The man had to talk, once he got rolling.

"I had a larger point to make. Mainly that we are all so predictable, my friend. Charm, like evil, is encrypted in the genes. That's the title. Of my book. *Charm, Like Evil.*

"Maybe you can help me. With a decent publisher? I think it would be interesting to take this on."

"I'd say you have to talk to someone else," Harry says. "I don't have that much pull in publishing. None, actually. Specifically, I usually deal with movies. Documentaries."

"Documentaries?"

"Is it movie material?"

"I can tell you, from the outset, I don't have much respect for the film people. Nothing personal.

"This is art. Listen Harry, let me explain myself. We have a confusing relationship to art in this world, I'd say. Look at the Mayans. Do you know about the Dresden codex?"

"Actually, I—"

"I happen to know where to find one of the codices. There are only three known. You won't believe when I say the one I speak of is the fourth.[3] Maybe I can show it to you.

3   The Dresden Codex's pages, in their brightly colored logograms with the modeled, varied line weight of present day cartoons of half naked warriors and partially decipherable glyphs, were considered blasphemous in their so-called pagan imagery, and had surprisingly survived Bishop Diego de Landa's self-righteous fling into the purging fires of 1521. Somehow the codex was delivered to a cloistered, protected shelf in a Dresden cathedral where it sat for several centuries. It was "discovered" there in 1739. It warranted little interest, perhaps mild curiosity, until 1829, when it had been erroneously attributed to the Aztecs. During the firestorms of World War II, the folio suffered subsequent despoiling. Surrounded in the limestone caverns of a Dresden cathedral, the codex soaked in a waterlogged cabinet while the city burned and fell around it. The seventy four pages (39 leaves with four blank pages) are rendered on amatl paper from kopo tree bark (also known as the sakewa tree; Latin name, *ficus centinofola*) finished with a fixative lime paste. The folio contains ancient rigorous astronomical calculations and the first gleanings of a 360 day year cycle (this year was known as a tun, of which a day was called a kun), and was one of the three known Mayan Codices believed to be sent from Cortes as a tribute to the King of Spain, after his taking of Mexico. In 1880 Ernst Foerstmann made a heavily annotated facsimile

"I have nothing against film people. Don't get me wrong. But an important, a significant story, a life story, is not to be contained in a two hour film—of constructed cause and effect. The oversimplification. Just to make us forget our own lives."

Malatesta walks to the edge of the patio. Harry remembered such supercilious men from his youth. Like the door to door salesmen who knew of his father's dry cleaning business and showed up to deliver a clever sales pitch with false confidence, usually when Harry was looking after Sophie. A man driving a Mark V leaving a brochure about a revolutionary new dry cleaning process. The man could barely make a living for himself, peddling junk, and looked like he was scraping to support his family.

Malatesta reaches into his pocket as he looks over Harry's head toward the door.

"The guest studio?" He hands Harry a key. "You look doubtful, but you could ask anyone here. Full disclosure. That piece you'll see? Well, bear in mind it's already months old."

Harry spoke up. "Actually, Frank—if I may call you that—I'm curious if you know what this is. "

Harry unfolds a single photocopied page he has been carrying with him from the box of archives and holds it out to Malatesta.

---

copy using chromolithography. Villacorta and Villacorta made another copy in 1930. The original remains under protective glass in the Staatsarchiv in Dresden.

# ROBERT DETMAN

<u>Agence International France Presse</u>
PARIS     RABAT     LONDON

63 rue de Vaugirard
Paris, FRANCE 7500
tel. 02-78839-8839

c/o Nathan Thomas
12 June 82

Frank:

    It pains and annoys me to have to say this. I know I should appreciate the efforts that you took to bring my father to me when it was really far too late. I suppose there is a part of me that wants to respect the relationship that you had with my father and all. But the mess this put me in with my mother of all people—basically I had to lie to her in order to fulfill your duty. And I now have a few things I have to say.

    I have never once considered you a relative of mine, so don't assume it now. At this point in my life, your continued insistence on my father's plans for me seems ludicrous and manipulative.

    Please be aware that I am now cutting my ties with you. I will find a cold shallow grave before I will come back to your compound and come into your service, honorable as this might seem to those of my father's acquaintances who had the misfortune, like him, of having worked—coerced, let's just call it what it is—for you on your "projects".

    Do not forget what I told you--trust you are not the only one with support. If you try to contact my office or anyone affiliated with me, I will proceed with exposing to the world how your little plan was going to

One page. Whatever revelatory action Basher was prepared to take was a mystery couched in an enigmatic threat.

Malatesta reads it over, squinting through his glasses.

"That is to you, right?" Harry asks.

"The memory's not a file cabinet. I can't say I've ever seen this before."

Malatesta smiles and removes his glasses to rub, reflexively, the red bridge of his nose.

"Strong words. A messenger of Nathaniel. I should have known. Strong words. I'm not surprised. So, I suppose the question is, what would you like to know?"

"I'm guessing he was here. I'd like to know where he went from here."

"It's so long ago. But, he was here. Frequently."

"I didn't realize."

"Of course. Let me tell you—it was between his father and him.

He thought he was a clever one, Nathaniel.

"We were at Subic Bay together. Nathaniel's father, Parker. While Parker ended up doing head shots and Panama City crime photographs—gangland killings, tabloids, Nathaniel did him one, or perhaps two, better.

"Nathaniel got out and lived a bit. He didn't get caught up in money or power—that was not his thing. Well, maybe power. He didn't concern himself with what his neighbor was doing. You could make the argument that his father set the example that he wanted to live down—and Nathaniel could only do that by tearing his father down.

"His father had brought him to the world, but he didn't give him any guidance. But Nathaniel could never figure the world out without someone to guide him."

Malatesta set to a repetitive stroking of his dog.

"The last time I saw him was when Parker lay dying in the hospital. Parker asked me to find Nathaniel and bring him to Panama.

"I owed it to Parker to keep tabs on his son. His estranged son. After Parker began his decline, I became involved. Not having children of my own, I had always considered Nathaniel to be like my own son. One of the realities of our connection was that nearly anyplace Nathaniel worked, I had connections, I could make things happen. He didn't want to acknowledge it, but I was indispensible to him. How else do you explain, at barely eighteen years old, getting a photographer's job in one of the most prestigious and free to roam press bureaus in the world?"

Malatesta hesitated, as if sizing Harry up again, before continuing.

"I knew where to find Nathaniel at that time. Afghanistan. I was there for professional reasons. I trekked for thirteen days in the Hindu Kush mountains; I camped out. Saw the Bamiya Buddhas, long before the Taliban could touch them. Met their notorious leader—maybe you've heard of him. Eventually I found Nathaniel and suggested he come back to Nacon.

"He wasn't going into battle like a soldier, but he was getting tricked out in a flak jacket and fatigues with a press badge—as if this could exempt him from harm. That's what he thought. Showing up at the latest warfront, he had a mission. He wasn't the only one. To his credit, neither was he heroic about it. He was low key. Central America was on no one's radar at that time, nor is it much on anyone's radar now. And the prestige was in getting the dirty jobs."

Malatesta's candor silenced Harry.

"As much as I have probably, indirectly, been responsible for not preventing deaths in far flung lands by my own position, I was able to procure these interesting assignments. Afghanistan. Guatemala. Yet, for the work I have done, I don't think you would find any difference between the results from my hand, and those of someone who sets out to do evil. It's motive that I'm talking about. At the time, these deaths were an abstraction in the service of my country and meant nothing to me as surely as they meant little more than a job.

"I never set out to rid the world of its enemies.

"This is why I have turned towards the arts—Raleigh, others. Patronage of these artists who would likely go undiscovered in the world. I am more in mind of the communal spirit of the sixties—yes, I hated the sixties. But I didn't join the service to become a puppet. When I moved down here, I became a pacifist. I was beginning to explore, like our young friend; exploring what possibilities there were for me in this world.

"I was the intercessor and the peace maker—I was seeing to Parker's wishes, bringing Nathaniel back here. He was in a jittery state from the long overnight flight—first on a C-130 transport—we were helicoptered to a carrier, the Constellation, and promptly taken by a larger craft, where we rendezvoused with Nathaniel.

"I was there, Nathaniel was there. Maria was there, Parker's second wife. I didn't know Maria well. Dolores declined my offers to be present.

"Something in that sterile Panamanian Military Hospital air. Panama was appropriate. An odor of funereal flowers pervades where those two seas are conjoined.

"He sat down at his father's bed side. I left the room—you'd have to have gotten a first hand account from Nathaniel about what they discussed. Let me say that as the dark hour came near, father and son had brokered what I thought of as a reconciliation. A classic détente.

"Not knowing any more at the time, I intended to take Nathaniel under my wing; Parker had instilled his trust in me. There was no pressure. Nathaniel could stay at Rancho Nacon as long as he wanted—it was just another way station for itinerants—if he wanted. He had come to closure with his father; I believed in what I had seen take place between father and son.

"Looking back now, I see that I trusted too readily in the theatrics of that scenario. What I saw was role playing. Who was fooling whom here? I could not think about it in these terms and instead felt that what I had seen had been as much a reality as what Nathaniel had led me to believe. Having had my own failure in this regard—my family has long since ceased to impact my life—I was honored to help my friend.

"I had made a strategic miscalculation, bringing them together. On his father's deathbed, no less—Nathaniel would not let his father go in peace. They must have despised each other. How I must have upset my best friend. I thought Nathaniel was beyond a vendetta.

"He left his father in a state of agitation.

"The less Nathaniel understood about his father the easier it was to cut free of him.

"He realized that he was, however much he did not want to be, his father's son."

Malatesta seemed to catch himself in some genuine emotion for the two, father and son. Harry didn't want to interrupt.

"Excuse me. You can imagine my surprise when I received news of first one death, the father, then the son. That letter—does nothing for Nathaniel who was unable to answer for himself. I think you can see for yourself in the tone that he assumes my plans for him. I doubt even that Nathaniel had written that letter.

"Nathaniel was in such a hurry to get away then. And then his accident.

"To think about it, I can't say that we weren't all a bit bewildered after what had already taken place that summer.

"We saw the God-forsaken life support, but it was over quite soon. The violence and effort of every breath. Heaped upon this body. Why keep this up, you think. We had just buried his father. I saw that life go away. I don't, to this day, think of it as his end. As I come closer to it I'm convinced. It never ends. It passes. A kind of suspended presence that I can still feel in certain moments, in particular, uncanny circumstances. I sensed him passing before me. It gave me an awareness. Death is not the death of the soul, but the abandonment of the physical body. We look at this body and imagine the life, because we have associated the life with this body, this person.

"They all think Nathaniel was in hot water out of a desire to make a change in the lives of some villagers. To document the process as he learned in his photo school. He managed to fool everyone on this account. He couldn't stay in one place long enough to know the repurcussions of his actions, I'm afraid to say.

"I think there is someone else here who may enlighten you.

"If you'll excuse me, now, I've got work to do."

They walk half a mile to get to the bar, in the dark. Harry feels foolish, going for more drinks. Mayor's idea.

He tells her of his plans, to get to the village where his friend had died. To locate the scene of the crime. A quest. Tells her of his, Basher's, connection to the place. She listens. The story quiets her, she seems restless.

"Am I giving too much information?" he asks.

She steels herself and looks away.

They sit at the bar. Lightning bounces on the clouds, a clod of mud dissolving in the shallow tidal pools, thunder, an echo that sustains. In lieu of negotiating a faltering conversation, he wants to write the image. Precise details for the documentary. He imagines it. Distant mountains falling into the sea. That is the sound. Also an image. A switch flicked on and off; an indifferent god playing with the lights. His judgment clouds and becomes literary. These are merely notes, set up for the talking heads scenes.

Now they have nothing to say, whereas at dinner they had conversed casually, about everything.

He signals for another round.

"Listen," he says, "you're starting to make me uncomfortable."

She watches his mouth and puts a finger to her lips. He takes a sip from the tequila and places the glass on the bar before her, offers her some. She puts up her hand. Enough.

They descend through the gently sloping blackness without a flashlight, to find the way through the grassy trail, muddy, slippery, down to the dirt road, lit at the crossing road by a single flickering bulb, to Mayor's cabana. He follows the slapping of her sandals in the mud; otherwise, her silence, trudging along, a few steps ahead of him. As if this is all alien to him, he occasionally comes in close so that he can feel her radiating heat, reaching to touch her shoulder to remind her he is there. He feels he might be misreading her.

"Maybe I should go," he says.

He slows down, and turns, wondering if they are being followed by someone, Zagros, maybe, since he'd seen them talking together. The flavor of the place. She keeps moving ahead of him.

"Andiamo," she says, pointing forward.

She leads him into a thicket, a web of branches. Uncertain as to if he is the player or is being played. All the same.

Holding out his hand. "I can't see," he says. But she won't submit, drifts ahead.

Lightning illuminates a silver plain draped in low clouds over the Caribbean, casting the path before them in a shocked outline.

"You don't know what I want," he says, flatly.

She looks long enough to flash a faint smile.

What he wanted, he remembers. Certainly, for half a second he wanted her, for a brief moment on the beach. He had noticed her there, sunning herself, another guest at Rancho Nacon. She walked past him kicking up puffs of sand as he wrote in his notebook:

*You have touched this person, and your memories die with you.*

He tried to do the polite thing, to stop noticing her, to let her become the background of the place.

He looked up to see her moving to the edge of the water; she dropped her wrap at the last second. She seemed to lure him to the water only to swim away from him.

Outside the walls of the Rancho, they were actors in their roles, animals. Wordless exchange.

Later, as he swam far off shore, he watched her enter the water. They were playing a game of people half their age. Harry thought himself foolish. Light sparking the waves, her bronze skin a distraction. She surfaced.

She went headlong into the surf past him, her strong arms and quick strokes taking her away. Drawing him out to the churning waters, a sharp reef just under the surface. He waved as he approached her.

"No," she said, swimming away from him. Later, conversations and dinner. Malatesta said she could talk plenty about Basher. Far too much drink for clear thinking.

Wafting into the air is a scent of flowers.

He looks back into the darkness and she throws herself around him, startling him; she clutches him, teasing, and then as suddenly pulls herself away.

"Maybe I should tell you," Harry starts.

She opens the door and leads him in to the overlit cabana; a young man carelessly cleans the rooms—at such a late hour?—distracted by their presence. Harry watches Mayor give the merest acknowledgement, innuendo, sending the man away. Harry calibrates the scenario. She knows him.

"You live here," Harry says.

Switching off the lights, she lights a candle.

She walks into a back room, into darkness.

He picks his way toward the light.

The room is a gauzy brown dimmed by guttering candle light. The moon in drift cloud sky. He reaches out for her. Leans in toward her.

Her hand brushes his hair, mild encouragement. He knows he is officially drunk, possibly unaccountable to his actions. He hears an animal cry out in the lone darkness, stopping as soon, the sound stifled by the thick walls.

He can barely see her face in the candle light as he feels her hands, her fingernails, pressing him down onto a chair.

Harry awakes, slumped on the chair, cast in pale light. The sun is coming up, brightening the room in steel blue, or perhaps this is an illusion. He doesn't know the time, guesses it to be no later than five, but he is not tired. He must have slept two hours. He senses Mayor's eyes upon him, her silhouetted figure in the wicker armchair opposite. She watches him, had watched him, for how long, he wonders, rubbing her stomach.

"Nothing happened," she says.

"What's going on?"

"You asked about him," she says. "Nathan. You couldn't stop mentioning him at dinner. I knew who you were talking about. You triggered some memories."

Her manner had been tinged with formality when others were present as he tried to make conversation on the patio. He thought they were both acting, conspiring, a calculated flirtation. He'd told her, *I don't know anyone named Mayor. Interesting name.*

*Americans think everything is interesting. It was a popular name in the sixteenth century, where I am from.*

*You are from the sixteenth century?*

"Just how well?"

"He was my lover."

Basher with one woman. Unlikely. After observing the drama of Basher with Christiane (conveniently forgetting his own), he thought he had his friend pegged: lone wolf. Basher always had different women with him. All over the wide world.

She coiled up and held herself, as if to not disturb the space beyond the chair.

"We were eventually married," she says.

Basher married, maybe he had heard and not believed it when he heard. But he would have remembered.

She continued. "I've known who you were the whole time."

"You might have said something."

"I thought you would remember."

"Remember?"

"Paris."

"I don't really remember that much about that time. I got involved with some people. Some were his friends."

"I knew them."

Mayor jogs his memory. He has drawn blanks at various points of twenty-five years past. He recalls the photographs on Janelle's floors. Mayor is another one of many.

"Listen, I was a different person then," he says.

Harry had been lax in his recall. An Argentine Basher had doted on, a shy girl from Buenos Aires who looked down self-consciously when Harry attempted to talk to her in his faltering Spanish.

Basher had introduced them. Harry had been so preoccupied with Christiane during those heady days, Mayor was just another demure foreigner.

He might have assumed she was someone marginally famous. Basher got into a habit of dropping the names of the elite he had befriended, eminent figures that were part of the public consciousness. A very young Princess Diana—he'd photographed her around Paris—for example. Also the Pope as he tagged along on a private delegation to Vatican City, and later, the President of Egypt, two months before his assassination. Basher was given a ride in His Highness's armor plated limousine. This litany irked Harry after a while, so much so that another femme fatale (how he thought of Basher's women then, being inaccessible to him, or nearly so) ceased to register. The minor public celebrity of his friend had distanced them, though years later Harry began to see that Basher wasn't name dropping for self-glory; he thought Harry would find these figures inspiring.

"Hypnotic eyes," she says, "like our son."

Harry didn't know how to take this, like she was teasing him with it, a sudden shift of tone, something forgotten recalled into the air.

"What?"

"Nathan's eyes. They were hypnotic."

"You said son?"

Mayor is transported back there. "You know that somber look."

Mayor softens her eyes and face and tilts her head to the left. Almost a parody, an exaggeration.

"Yes, I know it." Harry recoils on the precision of her memory, hitting on Basher's languid, hang-dog features on command. In the genius of hindsight, Basher resembled something androgynous, pale-faced, flat-chested. Basher forever young.

This gentle look of deception and fiery charisma ingratiated Basher to all susceptible. Women, in particular, to Harry's envious recall, could not help but look at him as if through a distorted lens.

"I remember that manipulative look. It's the fellow we all fell for."

"Stop," she says. "Only I was the one to capture him. He used to tell me I reminded him of a film actress." She took a plait of her hair and stroked it as if this could convey the memory.

"We were easy together," she says. "He wanted to take care of me, yet he seemed so often lost himself."

"Basher the seducer."

"You call him what?" she asked.

"Seducer."

"No—that name."

"Oh. Some of us called him Basher."

She smiled at this. "Yes," she says. "You were close?"

"Yes."

"You loved him, too. No?"

Harry considered the way she said it.

"I'm sure not in the same way you're thinking."

"How am I thinking?"

"Why don't you tell me."

"Nathan would sit with me for hours—we used to stare into each other's eyes, we did not have to speak."

"He didn't know the language," Harry offers lightly, half-joking. As fast, losing heart, veiling his condescension. "Basher gave everyone their version of himself, uniquely tailored."

"Is this a criticism?"

"I'm just recalling him myself. Maybe trying to lose my illusions about him," Harry says.

"That what you tell me—you are telling yourself. You doubt it yourself, what your friend meant to you. Am I right?"

"Maybe."

"He was wise."

"He was young. I think he had a deathwish."

"What does this mean?"

"He wasn't happy unless he was pursuing danger."

"I lost everything when I lost him."

"It seems so long ago," Harry says. "Then it doesn't seem so long ago."

"Why are you so eager to discuss him?" she asks. "Maybe you are hiding something I'd like to know?"

"No. I thought you did. I thought you all might—be hiding something. I'm writing a documentary film about his life, that's all."

"No one writes a documentary."

"I do. I am. I have."

"Perhaps you might keep quiet about this, here."

"Why?"

"Someone may not like the idea."

"You?"

"It's possible."

At first she intrigued him, now he concedes to that bugbear attraction. Awakening in the night and sitting in a wicker chair, staring at him. He regretted his overzealousness, his misguided certainty.

He could see the logic of her suspicion. She was using what she had learned from Basher.

Harry tries to recall her as a young girl in Paris. A bit roughened since, perhaps, but having moved on, as if she was unflappable, as Malatesta had characterized her. He could not see that tender lipped school girl with the oily skin that he imperfectly recalled, wide eyed at the world Basher must have led her into. She must have been very young then. Basher entered her world at the most influential time. Just as he had for Harry. He could see this—it had an effect on her—a loss of innocence. Basher was a different person for her, and the circumstances were different. The tatters of innocence for Harry had just fallen away.

"As he was leaving," she says, "with just his shoulder bag filled with his cameras and wearing that damn jacket. And it was very humid that day. I tried all of my—what is the word—to get him to stay. I had a sense of the . . . danger, as you say."

The last person close to him and she has precognition to boot. He fought his cynicism.

"The worst," Mayor says, "was never saying goodbye."

He can see the life that ties her to his friend, can see her loss, her mourning. He imagined he was the only one to carry his friend's memory, the only one who continued to imagine Basher had occupied his life and remained there long after his corporeal passing. Mayor too had been, like Harry was back then, gullible and inexperienced and needy. Basher's life to him now had become invested with a symbolic, even spiritual, weight. Harry saw someone invincible in Basher, and more. Someone empowering whom he wanted to be connected to, and thus he had been beguiled by his own later disappointment, anger, and abandonment. He could begin to acknowledge it. In hindsight, he sees Mayor's perfecting of a backward glance. It's his, too.

"Wiles, they're called," Harry says. "Feminine wiles."

"What is?"

"What you wanted to use to get him to stay. Also known as the oldest maneuver in the book."

"I might have saved him."

Basher is not his alone. He feels in her idealizing an unexpected trickle of annoyance.

"I doubt that," Harry says.

"I think I knew he would not return. He was American, is all."

Mayor thought Basher was seeing other women; this would not have surprised her, really, she said. She had made an effort to find out. She had gotten friendly with some of the women at the Bureau and had even offered to pay them to track his comings and goings. She needn't have tried so hard—in one visit to Paris she had spied on him. He was with a woman, someone he'd been involved with, from the looks of their silent possession of each other.

"The moor," Mayor says.

This could only be.

"From the bureau," she says. "Obviously, he was screwing her, too. It did not seem to be casual, which is what I start to see us as."

"She wasn't with the bureau." Harry says. "And if it means

anything, I'm quite sure it was long over with her."

"Of course."

"No matter. You said you two were married?" Harry says. "When was this?"

The comment went unacknowledged.

"I left Nathan then, and returned home to Mexico City. He would meet me here—before it was the center, it was always Ferdinand's expatriate hang out—as Nathan would go South again.

"You see," she says with emphasis, "he has these friends everywhere. I don't know who. He leaves for the border and hitches rides.

"He had befriended a family, people from a church. A German missionary trying to establish a cooperative for the Indians. This friend got into trouble with the government. Young men were enlisting in the guerillas—Nathan wanted to stop that. He couldn't simply walk away."

"He wasn't on assignment?"

"I'm not sure. I don't believe so."

He'd not tell her of the documentary being made of Basher's life back then—the other one, from the killing footage—the Simon Rasmussen footage—perhaps Basher had never told her.

"You said your son—his?"

"Nathan carried around a fertility fetish from the Congo," she says with a laugh. "It was meant to bring him luck."

Mayor was a revelation of Basher's life, past glory, something Harry could not fully account for until now. Harry might have triggered some reversion for her. She chose to live in that past, and filled in another gap in Harry's compendium of Basher's life, or lives, as he comes to think of them. The complications of a nomad.

What Mayor admits to Harry adds another dimension to the

ambiguity of Basher's life on the fly. In an hour Mayor has shined a light on a new distortion.

Basher said his goodbyes his way, sending her off with a casual farewell—she says she was sure that he didn't realize she would get pregnant—well, for that matter, she wasn't either. Not a surprise. She was nineteen then, "not of society," she says.

But for the corroborating facts, he couldn't square up the chronology of Mayor's story. Basher's last day wasn't the last day that she had seen him. He could pick out details. It was futile to decode. They were simply more details. Basher feeling the pinch from an alluring woman wasn't a far stretch, really, but the way Mayor colored in all the self-satisfying personal details, this supposed son.

"Where is your child now?" Harry asks.

"Do you want to know the truth?"

"Please."

"I don't know. Of course, he's no longer a child."

Harry had flown down here to dig up the dirt. This was a kind of payoff.

She wanted something in return, he suspected.

"So you have no idea where he is?"

"Back in Argentina, most likely."

"This is unbelievable."

"Believe what you want."

"You aren't in contact with him?"

"He went into the army. He may have gotten himself killed, like his father."

"You seem resigned to it."

"I need to be realistic. I can only hope I'm wrong. Can only hope he returns to me on his own terms."

"Have you talked to his family?" Harry asks, thinking of Basher's mother. "Nathan's?"

"His family," she says with defiance and finality. "I am his family."

"I simply thought—"

"I don't want to meet them."

"Maybe they'd like to know—your mother-in-law—that she has a grandson."

"No."

"Did you know his—Nathan's—father?"

"Vaguely. Nathan never talked of him."

Harry catches himself, how he appears so involved in this life of his friend.

"What if I doubt your story?"

"Do as you like. Nothing can change," she says. "Maybe you should go, soon."

"Leave—here?"

"The rancho. I know where you are going. I will drive you down the road."

"What did I miss?" Harry asks.

"He thinks you are trouble. Ferdinand. You weren't clear on your reasons for being here. He doesn't trust anyone who writes things down. He doesn't trust anyone who knew Nathan."

"But what about you?"

"I'm different. Ferdinand thinks he controls me," Mayor says. "As long as he thinks this, he thinks I have told you nothing."

# V. PILGRIMAGE

If death has a color, it is not ethereal white, that virginal color of innocence, or the windswept ever after emptiness of that loss. Nor is it red, the blunt literary equivalent of the onrushing of blood, unstoppable, or the chaos of uncontained energy, like a muzzle flash, or a firestorm, more orange than red, seeming to offer light. The color doesn't have a name, or is the result of the swirl of many colors, especially those saturated, sun washed tones of a documentarian's news photo from 1982. All mixed together into a color more akin to and as indescribable as a storm sky. It is ultimately closer to a bruise, the flesh tone slightly marred, which implies as much as the obvious wound, carefully covered in powder to hide the results of the fall, the forehead, the impact, a youthful face, better yet to be covered and sealed and burned away. Perhaps then the color of death is ash grey.

The backfiring startles Harry and he comes to in a blaze of heat, face cooking. The sun is in the wrong place. There is a pain in his head, something more than a headache from gripping the rails on the back of the truck as they blew over washed out roads. A small knot, compressed and digging, a sharp metal bit, is grinding away at the crown of his skull. His hand hurts his scalp when he touches there. Blood has matted. Disconcerting. The motorcyclist is gone. His army bag is gone. Watch and wallet, too. His back is dampened from lying in the grass and with his head against a tree. The demon blink of tail lights linger on the edge of his consciousness.

    He stands and teeters and palms the tree that has been his bedpost.

    He lost part of a day.

    What he remembers:

    He left with Mayor before daybreak. Driving through the dawn, down the Sian Ka'an Highway he supposed, before turning off and slow going over rutted roads. Exhausted, he drifted in and out of consciousness. The shadowy depths slipped around him, curling arms like serpent tails.

*I'm not going any further.* Mayor said, just before she left him, *I hope you know what you're doing.*

He woke to the cold and disinterested whir in the trees. Damp back.

Too late to turn around. He never let himself get to the safe place. Safe place a mantra of Janelle's.

As far as he can see is gray dimness of a pearl morning. They cannot wait forever. Mayor drove a truck. At first he thinks this is her truck. As if she has played a trick on him. Not as if. She has played him. The dream consisted of a spirit communing with him from the past. A piercing look like the one from the unfamiliar.

Before they let him climb onto the back of the truck, he felt their piercing looks. He was a curiosity. They all three leaned to look at him. The driver made the universal hand gesture for *come on, pardner.*

He picked up that ride at the border. They drove him through the dawn, down a paved two lane highway before turning off and bumping over rutted roads.

He reconstructs a sequence.

He caught a ride with them a few hours before. They had no room for him in the cab, so he held on to the roll bars on the back of the truck and was soon made numb and sore from the rattling over craters and through ditches, lashed from branches slinging in his face as they plowed carelessly through the bramble choked road. He wanted to stop. They were rounding a bend, slowing, and he saw a motorcycle tipped over, just off the road, a young kid lying unusually still in the ditch with his head obscured by the grass bank. An opportunity to stop, as a drop of sweat trickled on his brow, into his eyes. He slapped his palm on the hot roof of the truck cab. Por favore. The driver craned his neck out and slowed down, calling out, Si? That kid, Harry said. Para ayudar? The truck driver skidded to a stop, and Harry hopped off. Before he even let go of the roll bar, the driver gunned the accelerator and left him standing in a tan cloud of dust. Hasta luego, fuckers, Harry yelled out. They carried away his green army bag which held a change of clothes, some loose coins, a notepad.

The kid was hurt. When he looked closer, he could see steady breathing, the barely noticeable rise and fall of his chest. Life affirming respiration. He didn't know what he could do, anyway, just wait. He sat down on the damp grass, in a lee of shade, waiting for the kid to awaken.

He fell asleep. The kid then knocked him on the head and left him for dead. Took his wallet. With very little money, he remembers, thankfully. Useless traveler's checks, as he soon learned. He'd kept a wad of Mexican pesos in his sock. Things he didn't think twice about until they were gone, his watch that he wore all the time. A twenty-five jewel movement that whirred with assurance. Worth how much he never considered. A gift from Janelle. Expensive looking; Janelle had impeccable taste. What use is time to him, now, he thinks, wondering if a concussion has affected his reasoning; he cannot recall the position of the sun. When he jumped off the truck around midday, he might have faced a few more degrees east of north, rather than what his self-assured internal global positioning calculation led him to believe. He is surprised at the error and annoyed. Or because he has been taken advantage of. He shouldn't have worn the watch.

This kid's possible reaction, feeling endangered, awaking as he did seeing Harry lying there, nearby, and, asleep, perhaps, he must have been asleep since he does not remember. He notices his pants are coated with a fine layer of talcum dirt that has been kicked up in the air from vehicles driving by. And no one stopped.

Harry could see Basher on this same road, twenty-five years earlier, with bloodshot eyes peering at him, watching his moves, ready to give the order, through the foliage. Except he knows the reality, or part of it, the benign suddenness, the unlikelihood of Basher seeing the scenario happening the way it did. He squints into the haze and can see the edge of the jungle. Basher pretended to have a mission, a selfless purpose. Just one more job. Harry's motives are always so self-centered. In search of the elusive. Glory in someone else's victory. The fate of a documentarist. Defeat. Financial insecurity. He came down here to get a little closer to him, if possible at such a long remove, to understand, to empathize with his protagonist. All with the goal of how he would begin to show the enigma that was Basher.

The emotional life shut off too easily comes back to flood the senses. Basher the weight of the world he has constructed. As much as this is in his mind as it is in the steaming veldt undulating. Or it is a placebo from Mayor's jeweled palm.

It could have happened differently. Blacking out amid the waves of nausea so that he'd wished his quick demise. Such that he lives not in one moment but the fullness of them all. That would be enough. All of them alighting simultaneous. He'd not done anything to deserve this comes from the limited belief in a higher power. Maybe he would like to believe. He has to brace himself and with courage muster. All is not about survival until that slipping of the tether. The notes for *Deconstructing Nathan Thomas* like motes of dust in his frenzied mind. He'd wanted to break the tradition. Reinvent a genre. Great plans scribbled on a napkin while undergoing Greenglass's skeptical inquiry. He felt humored, not taken seriously for some time now. At least since waving his flag at the Korean restaurant. Pet project. Sent him off with expenses as if he could lose him for awhile. How he played to too many masters. Short on results they tolerated him.

On Basher's trail he once met a civil servant in the Mourne mountains. He was humbled by the deliberateness of a life lived in the certainty of the sun rising every morning. He fought that project no matter. It all does not come so easily to him such that he doubts the certainty of that sun rising each morning thus is thankful anew. He could not have that pointless toil through each of five days in seven. Like his father. The Oedipal bears down on him like the monkey howls in the night. In his gut. The source of all victories. The man with four children and a wife. In his fifties, he drove a bus and went to night school for a degree in psychology. He mentioned the *Puer Aeternnus*, said the word *pure*. Always what someone suggested he do for his own good. Someone a significant other. Harry dropped his psychology since it did him no good. Someone was always questioning his motives. Quite sure this is the beginning of a path like destiny, though he does not believe in destiny and one sided concepts.

All the means by which he tries to reconstruct his repulsion to the idea of family. Those who have gone beyond are the only ones that beckon to him now. The dead his coevals.

An hour passed like this, unhinged rumination. Close to the scene of the crime. He is dubious if he will recognize the road, after the months of analyzing the video tape, decoding the State Department report, studying aerial photographs. Near some ruins. Things didn't change much down here. *On no ones radar then, nor much on anyone's radar now.* Mayor had given him a map, hand drawn. Creased and fallen into pieces in his damp pants pocket. Useless. The markings he could make out labeled this, or some similar, unknown road, fittingly, Camino Terminale, with an arrow toward the town, Santa Rosario de la something or other.

The impenetrable landscape is clotted with sticky, insecty plants; the stillness of midday heat presses him down. Feel of rain in the air. Clouds of mosquitoes flit over swamps covered with patches of green goo. He gazes down the dirt road, wending through the countryside, impassable for long distances by any means other than a four wheel drive, bordering a deep ditch with fat-leafed plants. These rustle, dusted with dirt, as the rare, rumbling vehicle passes by. A panel truck, wrenching and creaking through the ruts; a motor bike, careening around the turns. They did not see him.

He leans forward and the throbbing in his head amplifies, a thunder, each beat of his heart. His mouth dry.

He hobbles forward with a slight list, believing that he is going in his intended direction, toward the goal, the site of Basher's murder. Where in the wilds of Western Guatemala. Somewhere, on a road like this, years earlier. Getting involved in a civil war that no one could ever comprehend, children walking around with AK-47s.

The truck turns down the road toward him. The truck, his interlopers. A passenger, the old man. Where he stood and held on for his life, sits the motorcycle. The truck inches forward.

He is thirsty and hungry, imagining that hunger kills the thirst or vice versa. Thirst trumps hunger. He reaches into the depths of his trouser pocket for the plastic bag where with foresight he has secreted the last few painkillers for his knee. Drugs trump thirst and hunger. The doctor suggested he take all of the prescription. The tail end of a month's dosage, down to the last five. He takes one and inspects it in his palm, rolls it between his dirty fingers and making as big a gob of spit in his mouth as possible, he tosses the pill to the back of his throat and swallows. He concentrates on swallowing hard as the chalky pill sticks. A mistake. He gags, coughs. A blush of heat, a momentary wave of self-defeat, sends a chill down his back. He pauses to let the retching reflex convulsing his upper body pass. He pops a second one, no problema.

He will catch a ride from the next vehicle that comes down the road. Waiting for the right vehicle, who is he kidding? In the near horizon the Caribbean laps at the muddy jungle, he believes, never seeing it. Never hearing it. There is a lake in the vicinity. The idea of water nearby gives him supreme peace of mind.

The houses, few and far apart, look just as he expects them to. Built for utility, not aesthetics. Every man made thing awaits the day the earth will take it back. He saw ranchos from the back of the truck on a slow rise above the roadway, concrete columns and tan colored bricks on stone plinths with terra cotta roofs at minimal slopes. Some without terra cotta, just bundled palm grass. Huts of corrugated metal siding tied arbitrarily onto vertical posts. These peak behind fences of tree trunks evenly spaced with ribbons of makeshift barbed wire fencing strung between them. The wire embeds in the folds of the tree bark and the tree heals around the wire. The trunks create a wall. An occasional dog traipses along, owning the land.

Rain begins to fall. He leans back to catch some in his mouth. He sees a hut through the brush. Clothing strung on a line flagging in an imperceptible breeze. In this direction he moves, away from the road, wading through a damp bank of grass.

He waits and watches. Empty. Approaches under the canopy. He sits down in the shade on the small brick stoop that juts from what must be the front door. The hut is a strange combination of modern and primitive means with the barest regard for the integrity of materials. Mud and cinder blocks. The walls should disintegrate in a heavy rain storm, though they could be reinforced. The small window, if this is what it is, is covered at an angle with a rust caked REO truck grill. Might be a storage shed.

He stops and listens. There are disorienting sounds from the surrounding field, an arthropodan hum. He puts his ear to the door. No sound from within the hut. A shooting spasm from his knee makes him sit down. He huddles to himself and slips off the cinder blocks onto the beaten ground, curling up next to the wall. He fades in and out. It is good to be still. Uncanny well-being, otherwise, the drug's doing. Head hurting less. He could fall asleep now.

He considers going back to walk the road to hitch a ride after a break.

Better to contemplate a fixed unknown than a series, in this state. Best to sleep off the rest of the day and deal with logistics in the morning. The heat of the day will be freezing cold at night. His detachment from pain and unlikely ease with the world is too apparent. Mayor seems like days ago.

*I hope you know what you are doing.*

They took him some distance. He doesn't know if this is the same road he meant to take, or if he would even recognize it. The truck ride cut through jungle roads far off the main road. He couldn't hope to know a way out. His grandmother told him, watch yourself down there in that

Mexico. He smiles at this, somewhere in Guatemala. Mexico seems so long ago.

If he had to, if his life depended on knowing where he is, which, he has the barest inkling that it just might, he will never find his way back. He will just go forward. Mayor too, had warned him, or tried to warn him off this journey. He would not be safe, would not fit in. Harry looked like every gringo to Mayor, the same way she stood for every local to him.

He imagines the owner of the hut. A family. They would come around, they would help him. He would hear them and scramble, in all likelihood.

He walks around to the back, stumbling over a trampled pen with a wire fence, smells the sweet rot of an animal. The place has been abandoned. He expects to see the culprit any minute now. There is no other door to the hut, just a small single screen window, bowed out from the frame from the inside.

He can discern nothing in the grim dark inside, except the pungent stench leaking out. He walks the perimeter of the hut, with his right hand he keeps himself upright against the wall. The overhanging fronds brush at his head. Stopping, he reaches to his head again and without looking is convinced his hand is the size of a catcher's mitt.

He looks into a bucket with a lid half off, a water basin of some kind, he can see to the bottom. He reaches in and scoops some water—minimal floaters—ignoring the retching smell he swallows several palmfuls.

He walks around to the front of the hut, tries the door. Turquoise blue, latched from the inside. He debates the wisdom of forcing in the door. He might be shot. All would be pointless. Not as dramatic. Just over. He sees the videotape on an endless loop. Basher up. Basher down. Up. Down. Your own death can never be as poignant, as eventful, as it would appear to others, out of a context. He thinks this way having turned Basher into his death, an event. A flailing protagonist.

Harry awakes, hours or moments later, to the loud chirruping of insects. The rain has stopped. The evening isn't as cold as he expected, the oxycodone eases the dominance of concern.

A low crescent moon in the western sky, smeared with swift moving clouds, casts a dim glow through the grainy shadow of the approaching evening. He touches the side of his head. Doesn't hurt so much now. He registers a sensory numbness at the limits of his consciousness, the promise of pain when the drugs wear off.

The fucking kid. Wasn't that big. He had terrified the kid who had an inclination toward opportunistic crime. Swung the bike helmet. Might have been afraid of killing him and only wished to do quick damage. Falling asleep saved his life. Awake, he would have taken the scrawny punk down.

Just dropping off his bike there on the side of the road for a nap.

He held onto the rails of that truck for over an hour. Slammed around, he couldn't jump off, and he couldn't sit and so crouched down like an idiot, whipped and lashed by low branches.

Compassion, or curiosity, in the back of his mind. He might have taken the motorcycle, which at the time did not seem a preferable option to the truck. He should have waited at least until the next village. When he asked, the truck driver waved his hands as if he did not understand him. Comprenda? Harry said. Donde esta una ciudad? The truck driver looked at the placid old man in the passenger seat, maybe his father, and he shrugged his shoulders and cracked a smile to reveal yellow teeth.

How he had gotten here. Research. He asked to go away. He demanded it. Wish granted. He is a lone man on no mission on his back in the dark. The cold is seeping through his pants.

At least, hopefully you will have lived.

How Basher must have felt when the gun was turned on him, never seeing the bullets flying toward his chest at a thousand meters per second. Morose thinking. Fruitless search. He pines for the conversation that a day ago provoked him. Irritated him. Some decent human contact, some reassurance in the earth that sucks him into the fastness. The frustration of Mrs. Basher Thomas, he let his guard down. Her husband is what she called him. Why couldn't she have kept quiet. Or been annoyed enough to ignore him. Instead, she tantalized him. Blindsided him. He had been a fool for not recognizing her. Maybe he did not need to know—more complication. Would there be a way of following through on this new information? Impatient, he wanted to get on the trail. He might have been able to locate the place if he had done some careful pre-planning, been systematic. Better directions, a coherent map. The pain in his head comes back again, vague failure. Time yet to find the village where Basher was killed.

It was twenty-five years ago, uncertain about the chronology he could barely remember. Memories are all that make up life, in the end—memories die with death. Who could make an honest account, who could leave any legacy? Dead youth. Legendary youth. The young and the bold own the world.

He walks away from the temporary shelter. He must be so close, going toward this goal. He'd had one hell of a plan, nebulous in the midst of pain, thirst and hunger, and giant mosquitoes. And interrupted sleep.

He remembers fragments of a dream in which he'd gone back to a familiar building, rather, a long barracks-like compound. Maybe Alameda where they were tearing up and renovating the old military base, or a figment of a factory from his hometown in Michigan, or that apartment in Paris—contained between high walls, the facade could not convey the vast interior. They had kicked out everyone who wouldn't take care of the place, meaning, the low-income residents, the dealers, the ne'er do wells. In dream logic, a group of missionaries had taken the building over and turned it into a dormitory.

A set of headlights from a vehicle turn down the road ahead of him. A truck. Janelle had said, "Welcome fear." He was going to die some day, now or later, he can no longer control his imagination's extremes, considering what he'd already been through. He'd only understood their friendship after he did not feel its pressures. He had never been prepared for Basher's initiations, what once scared the crap out of him.

Christiane, a detour, elegance concealing a fractured psyche. Harry's uncertainty came too late. Basher wanted something from him, enlisted his friends in all of his disputes. Harry, at the time, was a repair job. He appeared a freshly painted facade.

The light coming up turned to purple the beachy haze of morning—like all those summers in Michigan, when childhood couldn't conceive of adult-life, just an entire day getting waterlogged in the lake. What he'd like is a drink.

The truck stopped—his interlopers—the same truck that dropped him off yesterday in the bosque. In the back of the truck he saw a motorcycle, of the kid?—he saw a passenger, someone. The kid? The old man. The truck stopped, gunned forward. The driver saw Harry. The prickly flare of mutual recognition. He might have come back looking for him. The driver's arm dangled out of the truck, waving with casual interest. Sinister. Harry took a defensive stand, or managed to fake one through bare will-power.

The man calls out to him. Sounds like *Sahib*, but could not be. Trouble began as soon as he let Janelle fall out of the picture, the song began to waver, sped up, skipped, a Cuban drum, a minor piano chord ratcheted everything up a scale, a half note, jarring, repeating, like the rattle of automatic gun fire from a modified Kalashnikov. The painful interludes, questions as to the sources of happiness. Had he been swallowed in the breach of the earth, he'd seek pain-free memories and perfect, dithyrambic sunsets.

He'd lost pages of handwritten notes in a small paper-bound journal, maybe left or taken from him. Malatesta, who had also relieved him of Basher's photocopied letter—only the first page, at that, all that he had. The real meat of a story, snippets, overheard conversations, intuitions, violent dreams and night visitations; writing down the inexplicable in fear that he would forget. Now gone.

The truck approaches him in low gear, the driver concentrating, bumping over the hills and ruts of a ridge. Crossing perpendicular to the road. Harry stands on what seems to be a tractor trail, two worn tracks in the grass, far off the road. The edge of a neglected farm. The truck seizes up and stops, and then, with a gun of the engine, the wheels raise one side and the chassis humps forward, landing in a hole. Harry sees the face of the driver, sheepish, entreating, as the man gets out of the truck. Harry should tell him what to do. The man has something in his hand. A cellphone? He speaks in English—for you? could it be—the man is telling Harry there is a call for him. What are the chances. The man said, Harry. The man idled the truck and got down, up to his waist in grass. He held the phone toward Harry, shaking it as if Harry were inconveniencing him. That could not be a phone. No signal down here. Why should he have one that he now slips into his belt.

Harry looks closer and it is not a cell phone, but a small fold-up knife.

The man has come back for him after driving somewhere yesterday. They let Harry out because he wanted out, and now the man has come back to take him to the town.

The man straightens himself out. He is draped in a large safari type of khaki shirt, dulled through wear and harsh launderings. Button down pockets full. The harmless look of the man with a backwoods executioner's sartorial attendance. His jeans are too long for him, rolled up flares. Huaraches. Negligible in the mud. Thin moustache. The mode of the third-world, the dictatorship, the backwater. Coffee skin. What is it about the knife?

Harry waits, not wanting to show he is desperate for assistance from anyone, but the prospect of a ride is key. The man talks, but makes no sense. Not Spanish. The man is imploring him to get into the truck, he can tell by the gestures, that of all the alternatives is the sane one.

"Can I help you?" Harry says.

The man stops and looks back toward the truck. He puts his hand on the knife in his belt, as if unaware of threat-making. The man lifts Harry's green army bag from the passenger seat like a flag, to say, come and get it, if Harry will help him. He looks to Harry and makes the sign for driving, makes a motion to indicate movement forward, his hand a pointer toward one of earth's poles. He makes a more emphatic movement with his body, leaning against the truck. The truck, stuck.

At a distance of sixty feet or so, Harry watches. Encased in a mild throbbing, the injury to his head is not fatal. The painkillers have done their work. The hand reaches for the head, straw-like dirty hair, and a pressure on the skull where the hand touches, even a tickling, the fingers are one and the same, sensitivity spreads out on the pads of the fingers, the brain tells the hand to feel for the injury, a divot in coils of matted hair, how bad can it be when you cannot find the injury. Careful to not disrupt the wound the painkillers have allowed to elide for survival-sake. The man eyes him. Harry ventures some Spanish.

"Paseo?" Harry says.

The man smiles.

He can see that the old man he thought was a passenger in the truck is a gun rack with a coat and hat hanging from it. Or perhaps there was a passenger. The man invites Harry to take the passenger seat. Harry stands and waits, the man indicates for him to get in.

"Will you take me—" Harry says, pointing, trying to recall the words. *Ciudad. Camino.*

The man shrugs.

Harry reaches into his pocket for the map, pulls out a tattered piece of it and stops himself.

The man watches him.

"Camino—eh, to town. A la ciudad?"

The man nods and waves his thumb to the truck. Harry sizes him up. He is about five six, one-fifty, one-sixty. Non-threatening, size-wise. He might have had nothing to do with the attack. The man would not have come back if he was complicit in the criminal rolling done to Harry earlier. Harry points to the motorcycle.

"The kid?" Harry asks.

The man points to himself, taps his chest with emphasis.

"Usted?" Harry points.

The man nods. "Si."

"Uh, the kid. Muchacho—usted sabe?"

"Si."

"He took my money," Harry says. "Someone. Took my money. Mi dinero."

The man nods, Harry senses the man doesn't understand a word. The man points again to the truck.

Nothing.

Harry decides to get in the truck, preparing himself to run, fucking run, if necessary, at the first sign of the man's posse. He steps over the humps of ground, sinking into the muck. He sits down in the truck.

Harry sees the sparkle of an expensive watch on the man's arm. Harry's watch.

The man is wearing his watch.

The sense is immediate, if sentimental. Harry wants his watch back.

More than he wants water. He wants the man to come clean. Get his wallet back. They got him to the point he is now at. He had insinuated himself into their lives, convincing them to give him a ride. And he would give them something for helping him, sure. He did not doubt the injustice was clouding his rational thinking. They were justified in being suspicious of him. He had nothing more to offer. The phrase *ultimate sacrifice* comes to mind. And Basher. Having nothing to offer had done him in. The alarm Harry carries around like a tickling feather in the back of his brain is out of time. The situation, he must remember, was different under Rios Montt.

The feather in his brain moves into his throat. It tingles, and he heaves. Coughing, suppressing coughs.

Harry gestures to the man for water, frantic.

"Agua?" he chokes out.

The man reaches under the seat and pulls a plastic jug out. Harry nods. Grateful. He doesn't examine the water closely, unscrews the lid and gulps a quenching sip and imagines a salt rimmed margarita. The water on his throat is incomprehensible. He could quaff it all down. He gulps more than etiquette allows.

The man stuck the truck in gear and looked out the rear window, trying to see a way to drive it back to the road. The man presses the pedal and the truck lurches rearward. Harry is relieved to sit down, although he can feel the wire springs through the cracked upholstery. The seat is old but cushioned at the edges, and except for that, the truck is loud, what he did not care to notice before, too busy hanging on and dodging tree limbs. The man eases the truck, by increments, to the road. He turns out of the rut, and the front tires slam down hard into a rift. He guns the accelerator and shifting gears he rocks the truck backward and forward several times until the wheel rolls out. Harry watches him, urging him on, as if this helps. They emerge rear forward, squeezing through the thick leaves like a birth onto the road.

The man turns out the truck and accelerates. The truck backfires and shakes, but moves forward. Harry leans out the window, the breeze a relief billowing against his forehead.

Harry wants to understand. He wants to believe that because the man is letting him ride in the truck, he does not perceive him as a threat. Harry the turista who asks too many questions in the wrong tongue, is harmless.

Each perceiving the other as a threat.

Had they made some kind of traveler's pact—an understanding? Had the man not understood Harry's anger before? Perhaps he got conked immediately, and they waited ahead while the kid relieved Harry of watch and wallet.

There is water in the distance, a lake of some kind.

The man speaks; he makes a point. A rhapsodic elaboration.

Harry doesn't understand a word, but nods.

The landscape resembles some long drive into the middle west, even a lake he recalled seeing outside of Gram's hometown. Brown reeds in the shallows peaking up a flooded plain, still water, gun metal, an African horizon, a savannah, a civilization surviving on ruddy water. The edge of the Chicxulub crater's impact might have reached this periphery. These ponds and depressions were ancient. Michigan formed when a glacier melted away a mere fourteen thousand years ago. The sun warmed pockets of glacial melt caught between earth hummocks yielded the Great Lakes, so named when the native islanders starved, perished and learned to heed their winter shores.

He'd always wanted to go to the African savannah. Africa, though full of random boundaries, was boundless. In places it might even resemble Central America as the once immense Pangea had crooked that amphibious continent into its curling tendrils, sixty million odd years not withstanding. Where the two plates had found an edge, a river, a sea in common, once. At one time a simple undiminished mass of land with single celled organisms swimming around awaiting their division.

The man speaks.

It isn't Spanish, is more likely Maya, one of the myriad dialects: Cholan, Yucatec, Huastecan, Quiche. The man seemed to know or understand some of Harry's meager Spanish, at least enough for halfway convincing communication.

"No comprenda," Harry says.

"Perfecto," he says. "Mi nombre?"

"Perfect," Harry says. Harry points at him and says, "Perfect?"

The man nods.

Harry says, "Harry," and points at himself.

The man glances at him and with a gesture of his hand dismisses his talk. The man points again. He makes a figure with his two fluttering hands. Birds.

Harry looks in the direction of the lake. The land opens up as they leave the jungle behind, rolls out to fields, with clumps of trees here and there. Land the color of straw under storm skies. Purple hills on the horizon.

The man flicks his hand, Harry sees his watch again.

Harry impulsively points to the man's wrist.

The man glares at him and speaks under his breath.

Harry points to his own wrist—and encircles his hand around his wrist.

"That is mine," Harry stammers, recalling the word. "Reloj. Mi reloj."

The man shakes his head. He slows the truck down, and gesticulates with his arms.

The man looks pained, yet thoughtful, as if he understands Harry's words. The man responds, a rapid fire of flipping vowels and consonants, a stream of singsong. It shows a lack of understanding on his part, Harry reasons, that the man should know that Harry could not begin to know what the hell he is saying. But the man keeps talking. He looks to Harry every few moments to see how he is taking the words. *I will deliver you to the civil authorities.*

Harry had read, in preparation for this venture, of the lawlessness of Guatemala's bloody civil war. The gun rack was there for a reason, for the specious acquisition of personal affects. *The authorities will hear your request.* Those eyes saw thirty years of civil hell, took part in it. Torture was the mode down here. Like a legacy of the Maya, who were keen on slow dismemberment, jaw and finger removal. Methodical and trenchant blood letting, among other treasures.

Perfecto makes an effort to complain to Harry—what Harry takes to mean that he has no business suggesting the watch is his, which Harry further takes to mean that the man does not know that the watch is Harry's, only that *el muchacho*, his son, had somehow gotten it, found it worthless, and thus the man took it for himself. A legitimate appropriation. Agitated to explain, Perfecto keeps at it.

Perfecto stops talking and smiles. He laughs. Harry studies his baring of teeth, and laughs with him. Harry is almost convinced that the man may not understand that this is his watch, that the gift may have been earned, somehow, in his mind. Harry points to the motorcycle.

"Motocicleta?"

"Si," the man says.

"Su motocicleta?"

The man shakes his head again. The man peers at him through narrowed eyes. Harry turns back in his seat and lifts his hands to dismiss it. Too late. The man speaks again. Harry listens. He raises his hand again, not wanting to escalate, and stops himself.

The man drives and scowls. Harry doesn't want to press his luck.

He will wait for the town, a populace, cheap available food and water no problem. He'll trade if necessary. He was not going to act, not reach into his pockets, just keep to himself, get to the next town, make a phone call to Greenglass. Where the village gathers, so there is food and commerce. He should have learned the language.

"God-dammit," Harry says, unable to control himself. "You should just give me back my watch. *Mi reloj.*"

The man looks at him, squinting.

"Comprenda?" Harry says.

The man frowns.

"Forget it," Harry says. "Tiempo. Cuando."

He will end this madness in the town. He will forget the watch, the money, find a way to contact Mayor—the only one who might tell him where on the planet he is. On the roadway for a split second they pass Basher. Pure escapism. Basher at this moment could save him the trouble. This adventure would be a wash. He imagines walking into a cantina in the stark light of afternoon, the religious tropical light—so far inland, still, the air had the unmistakable tinge of the sea—and there would be Basher in a straw hat, playing a game of cards with the locals and speaking Perfecto's language. He would greet him, he would have not aged, of course, because Harry couldn't imagine his advancing in age. He was always the Basher of twenty-three, he would be no different. Perhaps, if possible, just wiser.

If it is necessary that one be comfortable in order to fall asleep, Harry could argue. Even if they have the misfortune of needing to sleep when slumped into a wire sprung seat, in a stranger's vehicle, in an unfamiliar country, the harm of taking the chance to close the eyes seems almost as slight as when driving down a highway in the desert at night and the thought of a momentary closing of the eyes will lend a pause to fatigue.

Bumps and jolts notwithstanding, Harry fights sleep.

The sky covered over with a sheet of dull plastic, torrid heat. He watches the landscape from the passenger side window. The shimmering backwater of some swamp, within a stones throw of the Caribbean. This notion keeps getting in his way, those aquamarine shades seem to be a salvation. He sees land and water moving through the squint of his eyes, drifting. Slow trudging on the beach, soft water and lying on warm sand amid the smells of sunscreen. How he had gone this far away, thinking about water, swimming in the cenote.

At the hut—he recalls opening his eyes in the half light of dawn:

horror. He took in the wood posts, the trampled path, the empty field bordered by jungle, an immense barrier to well-being. The brain making the movement of a leg for a leg that did not move. Then an arm. Immobile. A consciousness imprisoned in a body. A nightmare, close the eyes, go back to sleep, this will be over, soon.

He awoke to the portentous warbling of . . . a bird? . . . It goes thweeet, on a high swell, to a tapering tchk—tchk tchk tchktchktchk. Having heard the call in Costa Rica before, it was no less tentative in its unaccountable, benign charm. No one asks why birds sing. They were walk-ons in the Rasmussen footage. Rather, fly-ons. He'd never considered this before. In the slanting light, birds were irrelevant punctuation he ignored in the face of the main story. The sudden shots, the impact into his friend's body, recoiling. An explosion, the ripping of the fabric. The birds, startled, untucked their wings, dropped from limbs and stretched out, airborne with lazy ease, lifting off that dusty hill. From one bloody spot to another. So often it seemed like the birds were imitating airplanes, when in fact the airplanes were imitating them. Death didn't impinge on their existence.

Perfecto keeps driving. No need for conversation. Just the discomfort of trying to act normal under the circumstances. He recalled the trip to the Mourne mountains again, a land in tea stained blinding light, a sunburst evening. All the nameless dead-end islands, that breathtaking stop of the view: a sea painted backdrop, the town two rows of brown and white boxes lining the main street. He camped out in the woods on the leeward side of the hill, agitated by the martial drums of the Orange order marching through the town that night, echoing through a thousand feet. He happened into the field of the troubles. An abandoned car, engulfed in an inferno, melting into the pavement. Down there on the oil slicked streets of Portadown, Basher sat in a pub waiting for his contact—to be led to a secret meeting. The pictures were for a pop music magazine. He met and photographed some Orangeman, he was their voice. He would trust anyone to gain their trust.

Harry wanted to find out the name of that bird.

Greenglass suggested packing what might have come in handy: the cellphone, several credit cards, traveller's checks, just in case. If he could afford it, hire an interpreter. Mayor could have been useful. All had made for a convincing personal mission whose point is elusive. He couldn't enlist anyone for this without lying. He didn't have the heart to lie.

The numbing drugs dulled his pain enough that he felt disconcertingly good about it when he awoke that morning. He had been able to forget these practicalities and plug onward like Sisyphus. He made plans. Because if this began to resemble a vacation, there would be nothing noble and more pointless than to continue on.

Perfecto drives eerily slow. He is lulled by the wheels on the gravel. At the edge of plaguing thoughts. In meditation he had learned to let thoughts go, to not stop them, just let them go. His watch would function as a mnemonic, thinking he could hear it ticking, a good will gesture, an offering to the gods, a tribute, as the Maya used to make, gold and jade and maize.

Surrendering to the cocoon of sleep.

A room the size of the world ending in six depthless voids. Now his hands are large somnambulist puppets threatening to fill the room. Thoughts equally crowding for attention.

Once, with his entire family on a two day long drive to Florida. Stopping in Kentucky. Morning mists veil the blue grass. On a rise he sees a horse with a stately apparatus unleash a hot stream steaming onto the hoarfrosted grass. The milk for their box cereal in the camper trailer glazed over with a crust of ice. He learned what better-off was. A skittery family with their wild-eyed appeals, hungry, broken down on the highway. An Eldorado with irreparable rust patches. His father is the spirit of compassion that mother and son back away from; he will do something. Offers them not one package of Pop-Tarts but an entire box. Five kids like hellions bound out of the car. As much enmity his father has earned evaporates in these selfless acts recollected.

The truck bumps hard.

His family getting lost was so easy then that he wondered at the reality of being lost. His mother on a mission of avoidance. She could fool a group of children but were they all fooled? He sympathized but resented his acuity to watch the fuel gage leaning southward wondering to see how long she could stay clear of his father. She tells them that they are lost while she pilots the car through empty turned fields and thistle swaying as they pass. Winter Michigan. His world began to implode. Unravelled. Leaving them to wander and reconstruct a future until. Not a day passed when he did not recall her. The things children did to regain control of their world . . .

Harry had once had an instructor in high school warn the class against this kind of somnambulistic reverie, that it was a sign of lazy thinking. Like breathing from your stomach, the teacher said. He made Harry believe that one should never be a lazy thinker or breather. For years after that Harry never thought about anything but how much lazy thinking he did. Or if he was breathing from his stomach.

Fully awake again. Perfecto wears an odiferous aftershave of the kind he remembers smelling on his father in those days. The product had been marketed to convey formidable manliness. The smell makes him sick. He needs to be off this ride. He has to get to the village once he can figure out how to say the name. Starts with a T.

Ahead, a station wagon is parked sideways on the road. A man stands in the road waiting. Troubling. He wears a blue bandanna across his face. They could go around. The man stands and holds up his hand like he wants to ask for directions. Behind the car Harry sees a short man or boy, face also obscured by a bandanna, with a Kalashnikov. Popular model, AK. And a machete in his belt. As soon as he registers danger they bound full force toward Perfecto's truck. That sudden rush of doom. The gun aimed at him. The message is clear. He has invoked the dead in a novena. Evoked Basher's trail like destiny. What do they want seems to be the question Perfecto asks. Neither speaking a language Harry understands. Hobbled Spanish. Pork eh, Perfecto now responds. The men argue amongst themselves. The one with the gun puts the rough barrel in Harry's face and he flinches and leans away from it. One shot and this would be over so fast. The bile rises into his throat, a reason to fear the banditos. Time slows. A reckoning overcomes him. He has next to nothing to give them. His pills. No money. He cannot speak. He might have carried some trinkets with him. Something he could toss off and keep them at bay long enough so that they would let them go. When the man does not understand what he is telling him, Perfecto is jerked from the truck. Perhaps they do understand each other and Harry is about to witness an ancient Maya ritual road side boondoggle.

 Perfecto is strong armed and flung to the ground. Harry swallows hard.

 The man comes around and yanks the gun from the hands of the other and pushes him out of the way.

One gun among them.

The man swings the gun and aims at Perfecto.

The other reaches to open the passenger door and points the way for Harry. Compliant, he steps out.

He is grateful they do not grab him and fling him to the ground but at the same time, a bullet has no discretion. The man looks inside the truck and mumbles in the strange tongue. Perfecto calls out from the other side of the truck. They might know him. They might hurt him. They might intend to, yet.

He rifles through the truck. Digs in the glove box. Under the seats.

One takes the machete and slashes the already tattered, feeble seats. The machete is as dull as a butter knife. He pulls and rips the upholstery. Flapping over, dust powders the air.

They pocket their spoils. The knife. The leader inspects Harry's watch with a gleam in his eye. Satisfied, he slips it on his wrist and admires the sound, holding the face to his ear. Perfecto pleads with them. The man takes the keys to Perfecto's truck and hurls them into the brush.

Perfecto calls out again from the other side of the truck. He seems to be crying. One of the men comes from behind Harry and forces him into a sitting position. Execution style. He guards his knee. They hold his hands behind his back. The other patrols down the road and looks back to them. They wrap a sticky twine that seems to crackle around his wrists. Harry tries to keep his hands apart. The man doing the tying tightens the knot and holds him to the ground, reaches into Harry's pockets and paws around. He hopes they do not check his sock.

He notices the eye of the boy that had the gun, something wrong with it, milky, glaucous. The same height and build. The kid with the motorcycle.

They pull the plastic baggie with the painkillers out of his pocket and inspect it. Three left. One of the men asks him, What is it. Aspirina, Harry says, since whoever takes one won't know the difference anyway. A much stronger version of aspirin.

"*Aspirina fuerte*," Harry says. Take one with water until pain goes away, he thinks, in Spanish, then says, "*Toma una con agua para el dolor?*" The man sizes him up. From the eyes, he thinks that's a smile. He waits for them to hit him.

He wonders if his state of dishevelment might make him pathetic and immune from further punishment. He hopes. They check his pockets again and finding nothing of value seem satisfied. They do not check his socks.

The man pockets the baggie and leaves Harry sitting cramped by the side of the truck.

A shot goes off on the other side of the truck. Perfecto screams. Harry believed the ambush a con until that shot.

Perfecto whines. The continuity of the cry.

He was not shot.

The men argue. Fearful intonations. A ridiculous ending. All slows down and stills in his mind. He goes far away. He has control of the outcome. He has willed them from the jungle. A test of fortitude. They are a product of his disturbed mind.

With a certainty beyond knowledge. He knows. He knows they know he knows they will not kill them. He will not allow it. End of episode.

Under the truck he can see that they did not shoot, nor tie up,

Perfecto. The one with the gun, the leader, waves his arm (with Harry's watch) high in the air. The men climb in their car and turn to look back at them.

He waits for the man with the gun to take shots from the back of the car. He swings the gun back and forth at them. Harry keeps his head behind the ajar truck door. The boy stares back at him. The car pulls away. Silence.

Perfecto lies on the ground and weeps.

Harry calls out, "¿Mi amigo, está usted vivo?" That my friend is bullshit.

Perfecto whines.

Knee pain, just a bit, from the way he was forced to squat down into a cross-legged position. He does not move.

Emboldened by the experience.

He recalls the whole event. Five minutes. He saw two men but thinks there must have been more behind this. Perfecto is quiet, or Harry can no longer hear him.

Perfecto lifts himself up and brushes off. Methodical. Like a cat. He picks his hat off the gravel and spends a great deal of time pawing and patting the dust away. Harry watches through the truck cabin. Perfecto does not look over to him. Harry moves to stand up but with some effort. He strains with his bound hands. He wonders if Perfecto will help him. Perfecto stands inside the door of the truck and inspects the interior of the cab. Expressionless. He seems to look past him. He avoids Harry's eyes. Harry says, Perfecto. Perfecto glances at him. Harry has worked to slip his bound hands. He has them free and he twists his arms a bit in the effort. The twine falls away.

Perfecto stands shrouded in brush looking for the keys to the truck. Harry, still lost, is no further along than where he was twenty-four hours earlier. Perfecto looks to Harry when he cannot find the key. Don't look at me. Perfecto curses. Serves you right, Harry says. For Perfecto, the day before had not gone as planned. Ensnared in some vendetta. Men are like boys with guns.

Harry sits up on the running board, buries his face in his hands. A slight tingle in his knee.

A hand on his shoulder shakes him. Seen-your. Seen-your. Perfecto, a shroud of greasy hair, two palms waving above a wax visage.

Perfecto looks at him. Perfecto stammers and twists. He takes Harry's arm, a snake slithering.

"Get off me," Harry says. "Not my problema! Comprenda?"

Perfecto backs away. He looks in his eyes. Harry might help him. Harry has an escape. Too soon for his bones to become the road.

Harry walks. Just go away. Get out of here. Find the fucking town.

He walks on the sundusted road. He will not look back. He hears Perfecto's troubling queries, fading away.

He walks, knee atingle.

His thoughts the voice that everyone carries though no one mentions. A second person talking to him because it seems ages since he spoke with anyone. That voice of reason that he employed. That voice kept him company in his thoughts when he built everything on memory. Memories and words to reconstruct an altered picture of the past. There might be a grain of truth to what he avoided about his friend for so long. And yet, Basher was no suicide in the proper term of the word.

Seeking signs in the lethargy of unknowns. The unknown makes a mockery of received ideas.

In the face of no alternative solace in the last, he lusted for Mayor.

Real or imagined. All the same in memory. Dropping through the dark hills night trembles. A slipping foot in the dark. No light to see but the flicker of a thunderstorm. She prided herself on worldly victories. Not the only one. Not the first. Not the last. Slap of sandals in mud. A warm hand taking his own. Could be any one. No warm hands now. Just the feverish clutch of bramble in his own claw. Need of food again and a shower. A warm body. A warmth from the loins as it traces along his spine.

Just a little out of it. An empty road stretches ahead of him.

The killer comes loud and makes demands. None of this matters. Silence the burdensome words. All is not lost or all is lost no matter which. Approach the easy prey. Snakes sliding in. The pain of living alleviated by sheer survival. In the night he felt her coiling around. Cannot now be sure. Saw it for certain in his mind's eye. At least his mind. And ears. As it was in the beginning so it shall be in the end. Death the man in the hemp hat and grime stained trousers. Family a symbol of what. The pain not necessarily any worse now.

Road signs. A town coming into view. Focus, calm.

Guilt, of course, in retrospect. Leaving him, Perfecto, without a second thought, helpless by his truck. The truck Perfecto could not escape. Who was to say that they had not come from that very town. Maybe an hour and a half walk, perhaps ten minutes in the truck. Perfecto could come looking for him, Harry, after all that. They knew Perfecto. They knew where to find him. He'd hoped that would be the last his eyes would ever see of Perfecto and company.

Yet, if he thought he would not run into him again, he would not have let his watch disappear like that. He turned that hunk of noble metal into a symbolic item that he could focus on. The watch was the salve that he could use. The pain in his head comes back again, a vague sense of failure.

Still, he will find the village where Basher was killed if it kills him.

# VI. OFFERING

The scene is set up for the video camera, for the unofficial documentary that Basher hadn't told anyone about. There is an air of artificiality to the set, with one cameraman and some back-up lighting hooked to a generator in a truck. But the players are real, that gun is real, the circumstances all of a sudden, uncertain. He hadn't thought this would be a feature film, not only because he doesn't think his life's story merits it, but because there are no directors and set people standing around with klieg lights waiting for noon when they can all race to the lunch truck. And he knows or thinks he knows this boy and that this boy has a gun that looks strikingly like all the other Automatic Kalashnikovs he's seen. He has, after all, always been trying to reveal what he doesn't know through his work, what he safely hides behind. He does not want to be the subject because that will allow them to question his integrity. He doesn't know the feeling of seeing himself suspended in celluloid, the grains of his being transformed into chromatic hues. There is Basher and the boy with a gun, an uneasy stand off. The boy who will be a man *someday and if the boy can make it happen sooner by the power vested in his hands, he will. In this soon to be classic footage he is still just a boy as boys will be, down through the ages, but a boy with a gun, facing him. And this boy pulls the trigger.*

Outrage. The public's sense when the footage airs. Frank Reynolds, silver haired, neatly groomed, with gravity and indignation saying, He's one of ours.

The sunlight lidocaine through trees. The temperate air Harry feels on his skin though like he's been getting it all through the footage. It's already got a bit of age and distance, it's pushing him back to where he was, what he was doing then.

Harry notices, after so many repetitions of the images, the moment when the light leaves Basher's eyes, when the sun shrouded sea turns gray, it's the moment he knows, twenty-three years in seconds, all that his friend lived up to, all that he simply did without thinking because it's what he had to do. It cannot be helped.

Yes, he's one of ours, Frank Reynolds says, seems to say, you wouldn't understand. What a miserable business this war. It pains me to contemplate this footage. These deaths happen every year but that only makes it more difficult to go on. As if he is talking about war like there is only one but there are many in that difficult year, 1982.

Divination. This is how he will explain, if anyone asks. There must be something more than voyeuristic curiosity that compels him, after all.

Harry can see how Basher gathered information constantly, as much for his assignment as to protect himself. He didn't think about his mother's worry, had effectively blocked it or flaunted it through his profession. If she knew what he had faced she'd have been terrified, horrified more likely. A mother who watches her son going into the ground, collapsing in grief. Basher's mother's memory was selective, it had to be, she had to block out the place names that appeared frequently in the news because the news from those places was the chaos of people behaving badly.

They could have gone anywhere to get live footage, Harry thinks, even, perhaps, Michigan. Or perhaps not, seeing the profusion of tropical foliage and birds, flitting into and out of the frames so adroitly that they too could have been enlisted for effect.

There wasn't anything to photograph in the village that day, most of the damage had been done and left to fester and Basher had gone there with Rasmussen for some realistic footage, some background of a place he'd returned to several times before, he had friends there and they looked upon this gringo with initial circumspection, until he learned their language, until he brought them a token of good will, or at least, this is how it would be characterized to Harry, later. Basher became familiar and they accepted him.

What animates the scene is less the death in a grainy arrangement than the sureness of the camera that does not lie, not quite steady, but trained in on the figure though the event is clearly not what was planned.

His invisible actions, to stay on camera, to intervene, to duck in danger, seem calmly implemented, even clinical.

And who knows what his camera man is thinking, but maybe this drama is all for his benefit?

His movements are awkward with a video camera trained on him. It makes him wary, like if he disowns his body he can shake it off, it makes his skin prickle, his movements controlled by some disrespectful magnetic force.

Or it's a veiled irritation at Rasmussen's stage directions, insulting suggestions that he look more photojournaley when he is about to go under fire—thus the kid with the gun is brought in for realism's sake. And it takes one second, and the kid doesn't know what he's doing or why he's being told to do this, all he knows is when he holds up the barrel like this he's going to fire it, he's definitely going to. It cannot be helped.

And like this the boy is acting a part with Basher, motioning him to his knees, miming it because it's clear Basher doesn't get it. The boy is asking him to hand over the camera but this is all a game suddenly, this part of the game Basher is beginning to notice isn't quite what he thinks it should be, he has his suspicions. He's not putting the camera on the ground and he's definitely not putting it in this kid's hands.

And when he drops to his knees, there is an element of playing along, of, just get me through this unnecessary annoyance, who put this kid in charge anyway, and, well, it's a pretty big gun for a babe so small, and . . .

His legs slump under, marionette-like, doing a dance to an unearthly soundtrack.

Harry hears it, the rapid fire rattling a distorted soundtrack. His friend hearing it was less likely because sound travels slower than the objects that begat it, and he's likely not feeling any pain as he's already in shock as his legs give out, as he becomes intimate with Guatemalan soil. And in seconds he is pooling, his life is running out like a crimson river to the sea, somewhere, he keeps flowing, or he's in the air, he's in the ground Harry stands on, he's twenty-three, now and forever.

Why he is here. Why he has come looking for the Village of T., a name scribbled on a crumpled piece of paper: *Find the place where Basher died. Simple. The village. Name starts with a T.*

He enters the edge of a town.

He walks past the silent halls and colored facades. A bone colored church cross. A change of light and air, as if he'd stepped from behind curtains. Empty facades with eyes behind shuttered windows. He might as well be naked, so vulnerable. An unfamiliar grid. He'd wander around the grid until everyone in the town will have seen him. He looks for a place to stay, *Sa rentan*. Two men talking in a doorway.

The church he'd passed stood in view of every corner. A prideful church with the European influence. Low slung earthen walled houses painted in chromatic primary colors, some aqua, some yellow. The zocalo a wide raised plinth with broken swingsets and vendor huts. The bases of trees are painted with lime, a white wash which protects from the sun, which in turn prevents the tree from becoming weak and susceptible to insects. An artificial sea level to ward off decay. They paint the base of buildings, plinth walls, churches, for uniformity, though presumably on man-made structures, to repel insects.

One of the men gesticulates wildly, his tone growing ever louder and more emphatic. The other fellow stays sullen faced and listens. All at once, the listener laughs raucously. Maybe they are drunk. In the states they'd be waiting for a van to arrive to take them to a day job. Not the most pleasant reckoning for him to make. Downright improper, perhaps. But not unrealistic, either. They stop talking when Harry walks by them. He wants to ask, Donde esta un hotel? but decides against it. He continues his walk around the square looking for a sign. Desperate for a shower.

The men resume their talk, as he has passed. He is the center of his own action.

Arriving in a new town, looking for lodging. No one at his back, but no one is looking for him, although he half expected Perfecto. That motorcycle kid and the station wagon would follow. An ordeal on the back roads that only happened in the movies, to be recognized and pursued, as if your personal business is anyone else's business.

There isn't much traffic through this town, a respectable enough town, more than a village, but nothing picturesque, nothing worth stopping for. He is disconsolate, if he is honest with himself. He'd take the corner of a room at this point.

Off the edge of the plaza is a doorway through a kind of cloister into a motel that looks like a house.

It is the first sign that he can see.

He pushes open the door. His life is about procuring rooms in exotic countries. He'll barter with those Mexican pesos.

A woman gets behind the counter as he approaches. As if she had expected him. She could have been coming from church, or going to church. Is it not Sunday? Tallying up the ledger.

Rosary and icons on the wall. Our Lady of Guadalupe in multi-colored metallic relief. The place is neat. Overly bright. Fluorescent and white surfaces shining all around. The astringent of sweet cleaning solvents in his nose. She'd been prepared for a customer. They'd been far too infrequently accommodating the odd gringo who happened to find himself down on his luck in the little unassuming town such that Harry is a prize.

One big window at the front. No other ground floor windows that he can see. The feel of a damp cellar. The too large lobby that might be the proprietor's living room with an old naugahyde recliner and a couch that might have come from his father's basement. A green bird in a cage regards Harry with caution. These caged birds tend to go crazy if they don't like something, so silence is possibly a good sign. Harry more than ever felt he was one of them, an animal.

He has to account for the scab on his head, although the injury perhaps isn't so visible, a small bump, some caked blood. He wants to conceal it. It doesn't even hurt now, except just when he forgets. He reaches up there to touch it.

She is dark and ancient. She has been waiting for him. Of course, she had been waiting for a customer all day, a hapless traveller. She seemed genuinely pleased that Harry picked her establishment, perhaps acting. Harry knew how he looked and smelled. She could be selective. Still, there is something unassuming in her behavior.

"Quiero alquilar un sitio," Harry says.

She corrects him, "Un cuarto." She spoke deliberately. "Quiero alquilar *un cuarto,*" she repeats.

He asks, carefully, "Cual es el nombre de esta ciudad?"

She shakes her head, does not understand.

"En donde estamos?"

"Si."

Clearly this is not where I expected to be, he says, to himself. She puts up her hand. She has a lesson to impart. No, she says, with a wave of her hand. "*Como se dice,*" she points at her lower lip or her tongue to show him how to mouth the words. Rather than annoying, he finds it disarming. She has not acknowledged that he looks like hell—perhaps she is used to seeing blonde gringos crazily wandering the streets looking for the town lodgings.

Finding someone welcoming made him feel like this is where he should have been in the first place. After that ordeal, he won't rest easy.

The woman smiles. Harry repeats her words, crazily convinced that he understands what she is saying. Say it like *this.* He says it again. She stops him with a hand on his arm and says, si. She smiles. She holds up a finger again and speaks slowly. Harry put up his hand—making a timid fist at his mouth as if to say, slow down please, I don't understand. She says, ah, si. Most of this is unnecessary formality, she knows why he is there. She goes behind the counter and pulls a key for him.

"One thing," Harry says. "*Una momento. Yo tengo mucha plata?*" He pulls out the wad from his shoe. It looks to be more than he remembered. Damp loose bills spill from his fingers. She put a hand on them to inspect, notices they are pesos and regards the currency with a frown. She waves it off regardless. He is in dire straits, she has to see the wreck of him.

She points to his head. Harry tries to wave it off. She reaches up and stills him. She puts her hand to his head and inspects the injury. She walks over to the sink, runs water and soaks the corner of a towel. She leads him to a chair and makes him sit. She squints carefully and dabs at the wound with the towel, gently—he feels cared for in a way he could not recall lately. He knows he can be emotional, and fights it with all of his will.

This brings them into an unusual personal space that after everything makes him begin to drop his guard. She can read in his manner and gives him a calming look. She notices he might cry. A hand on the shoulder. He can smell her, too, gardenia and a touch of perspiration. Grandmother again.

He can still hear the men in the plaza. The voices staccato like rocks being dumped in a bin. As coarse and gravelly. Some laughter. The sound of a vehicle starting up, loud, backfiring into the square. The truck? He imagines the ambushers going back and shooting the high hell out of Perfecto and his truck. Surreal. When an animal gets desperate for survival, to what ends it won't go to.

He unconsciously tunes the woman out.

He is best off to put them behind him. The experience has given him something to chew on. Getting the one hundred proof taste of Basher's sojourns. Of course, Basher had this experience, undoubtedly. But it wasn't anything he wanted to go back to. In the wrong place at the wrong time.

He will try to relax. Except for the barren and sand dusted quality of the place, everything here looks cared for. There is pride in these humble dwellings, pride in this town, the church not being the least of it. In every town like this the church seemed to be the centerpiece of the town, axial to the zocalo, the center of activity and rituals that collect the life of the town along with it. The stated order of things, a kind of safe zone, perhaps, he was in now. Everyone put their change in the collection box at the church. He'd long since been one of the fallen.

She leads him back down a fluorescent lit hall to a door. The door is paperboard thin and she pushes it ajar to show him the room. The shower and toilet are in the room, separated by a curtain attached to the ceiling. He notices the nozzle of the shower is missing. "Agua caliente?" he asks. Harry points at himself and makes a face and she assents with her eyes, the way a motel proprietor tries to convince you that the place is up to or above standards you are used to.

Harry hopes he hasn't made this impression, considering that he looks like hell. She made some comment about the toilet, hold it down, she seems to say in Spanish. He tries not to look too puzzled. She says it again, slowly. When she speaks that way, he senses he catches each word.

The lack of a nozzle will have to be overlooked. It will do. He doesn't much care. He wants to crawl under the spigot and turn it on.

She walks him back to the office counter.

He thought to ask her about the village. He notices a map on the wall and points. Where are we, he asks. She indicates an area with her grasping fingers, as if picking up a pinch of sand. The town they are in does not seem to be on the map, and for this she explains carefully, again, what is there and why. It is lost on Harry. No scale, he can't see where or how far he has to go, because he doesn't know where he is. He can't remember the name, written down somewhere. Starts with a T. He makes a T with his two hands.

She shakes her head solemnly, smiles.

Does she not know of a village nearby, name starts with a T? In

Guatemala? Si, he says. Guatemala. She points to the ground, taps a foot. We are here, she seems to say. Si, I thought so, Harry says. She holds up her hand again, as if to pause the conversation. She goes behind the counter and pulls another map out. She unfolds the white and green tableau and draws a line with the ballpoint pen across the map. She points her finger at an area, some distance from the red line she has drawn, perhaps where they are now. She says a name, perhaps in dialect, he can't really know. He repeats the name she says, trying to do it phonetically. The woman nods.

Si?

Her hand goes to her cheek. She is silent.

Does she know the name?

She shakes her head, doubtfully. She places her hands one on the other, as if in prayer, on the countertop.

He feels compelled to explain where he came from, or where he is going, since she is his first receptive audience. He mentions the truck he came in, in his mixed Spanish, but still she does not understand him.

Harry mentions Rancho Nacon. The woman smiles in doubt.

He says, carro, camino.

The woman says, ah, carro. Si, Harry says. He explains as best he can his plight . . . long drive over broken roads . . . getting robbed and left (as he points to his head) . . . sleeping outside a hut . . . hitched a ride with a man in a truck . . . yet another roadside attack . . . Maybe she knows them? . . . All that he can't quite put his mind around now. Leaving his story in the past where it belongs. He had passed an abused looking bus near the zocalo and thought that might get him down the road.

"Can I catch a bus to the town—village? To take down this road?" he asks. She looks puzzled. He says it again, more simply. "A bus to that village," he says, pointing where she had earlier. He waves in a direction outside, West, he believes. Si, she says. Si. Tomorrow morning. She walks over to the window and points to the square. He can see the bus stop. He could take that bus to the outskirts of the village where Basher died. Maybe he'd have to call someone back in California to get a revised bearing. Mrs. Thomas. He'd have to locate a phone, first. Why on earth are you there, Harry? Why the hell to any of it. He could not tell her.

After sleeping unexpectedly well on the lumpy mattress and showering under a hot stream of water, Harry had eaten the breakfast the woman had prepared, huevos revueltos with far too much salt, frijoles and black coffee. She had exchanged his pesos for him.

In the morning, the road around the square was slippery. It had rained once, a brief, shocking downpour for ten minutes, clearing the air of the bugs and humidity. Turning the road to a clayey mud.

He walked to the bus stop, past collarless dogs and a sign that said *lavanderia*. Past the church, past houses, squat square with two posts and a veranda, and corrugated metal roofs. Bare bulbs lighting their interiors.

He walked through the square feeling the town less sinister. Less a barrier to his goal than another place to have collected himself for the penultimate leg of a journey.

After pulling onto the road out of the town, the van driver slowed and called out to a young woman standing at the side of the road, in front of a hut. She nods to him and waves him on.

"That was my wife," the driver says. "I was asking her if anyone needed a ride."

Harry steps on, and is the only passenger. The bus driver's English is welcome to Harry's ears, but he realizes he is not in a talkative mood. He hopes the circumstances are not an inducement to conversation.

"There are two seasons here," the driver says. "Rain and clear. This is the rain season."

The van is a rusted, creaky Ford, years past its useful life, with Turismo painted on the side. Its frame measures out each bump as they rattle through the mud. This bus made a daily trip to Huehuetenango, he learns, there and back, trudging hundreds of times over washed out and meandering back roads.

"Where are you trying to go, my friend?" the driver asks.

"I'm looking for a village," Harry says.

"Huehuetenango?"

"No. It's not on any map."

"They never are," the man says. "You might want to go to Huehuetenango. There's not much around here."

Harry says what he could of the name. "It starts with a T," he says. "Not very large. I know it's around here."

Harry told him the story, that he was writing a screenplay based on his friend's life, that his friend had spent time here in the early eighties, avoiding the specifics. Stopping short of talking about his own eventful past two days here. To hear himself talking freely in his native tongue to someone who could understand, he caught himself in his certainty—a certainty that he really did not have. Making it all sound falsely assured.

Harry explained, however dubiously, that he'd seen the village on a satellite photograph.

The driver took in Harry's story and was silent for a length of the road. After driving for awhile, he stopped the van and turned around to speak. Harry perked up to this; he'd had enough of the odd roadside ambush. He had probably told him too much.

"What are you going to do there?" the driver asks.

"You know the village?" Harry asks.

"I believe I know. Yes."

"So I can get there from here?"

He considered Harry's request.

"Listen, my friend," the driver says, "I usually don't go that way."

"You can just let me out when we're close," Harry says. "And point the way."

After an hour of uncomfortable silence, the driver spoke.

"It's okay. I take you."

They came into view of a narrow road off the main one. The bus driver told him that he might have to walk a short distance, he wasn't certain how far, but no more than a quarter of a mile. There he would find the village.

"I come back this way," the driver says. "I will look for you later."

"I'll just find a place to stay here, probably," Harry says. "But thanks."

"No matter, look for me, I come back this way."

A small wave of fatigue caught him as the van pulled away. No one here. He heard a motorcycle in the distance.

What had happened to the kid who had killed Basher? He could be anyone he saw. He could have been one of the men in the truck. He could have been the bus driver.

Walking the path, Harry was beginning to feel the journey devoid of purpose, perhaps anti-climactic, although that wasn't entirely unwelcome. He wasn't sure what he intended to do. Being here, perhaps, would be enough. To see it, to touch the ground, where his friend's blood went into the ground.

This the place he should have come to all along. This the place he should have been when Mrs. Thomas returned with the ashes. But he had been stubborn then, or avoiding it, afraid of facing the reality then. Not wanting to turn Basher's death into a celebration, the way the gathered mourners said their piece, sprinkled a shovelful of dirt, packed up and moved on. This was not what he could have done.

A strange ambivalence had shaped his world as Harry had related to it through memories and twenty-five plus years: How we each are the other's world. Whose deconstructed Basher Thomas? The dead were innocent forever. The surviving never had more than the memories of that past, if they insisted in hanging on.

Had he insisted?

He was another day or so away from wrapping it up and heading home. And he wanted to return, uncertain as he was that he could find a way into *Deconstructing Nathan Thomas* again. He could almost always arrive at this conclusion after only a few days of travel, even under normal circumstances. Two days could seem enough.

To begin to try to recognize what he had been tuning out. To make a call to Janelle from the village, or wait. If he'd mention meeting a woman who claimed to be Basher's wife—would he ever see Mayor again?—she'd hear the fact of the matter all in his voice. He should be there to work on the damage.

To try to find a way to explain his story—by not saying much.

He'd not mention the lost watch. She might wonder if he had lost his mind, too. He could hear her asking. Change isn't invoked consciously as much as it is by a real, dramatic and undeniable surprise.

As for the Raleigh Dawes piece, give *Munificence* the story that they were expecting. He learned nothing about Raleigh Dawes. Try to write it so that it would just go toward the ambiguous *Deconstructing Nathan Thomas*. He would have to deliver something—or he'd be at the end with the project. It would be out of his hands, if it wasn't already.

Just how far along will he have to walk. He'd look in at their church, speak to someone. Basher's final stop.

He is certain this is it. Along the east side is a river.

The road had been heavily used, recently. A set of two tracks, trenches, were carved out through the muck, from heavy earthmovers. Not unlike the road he had been on the day before, but that this was the no name road as in the video. In the middle of a green map that time forgot. His skin is prickling. There is not a soul around. Through some trees he sees a yellow backhoe.

The unremarkable place Basher had returned to.

He walked to the end of the road, but could not see the village. He walked to where the road widened into unusual, sunbrightened air.

Harry stopped and looked around. Basher had fallen somewhere here.

Quiet. Not even a bird, no wind. Silence, as if the moment before the magnificent destruction.

Beyond the tall grass was a clearing. He walked in and peered closer. He thought there was a cemetery, but nothing.

The ground was a smooth plain of mud, leveled flat.

No sign of any of the huts he expected to see. Nothing of the church where they had taken Basher, just the ground from where he had been airlifted. Now all barren. Pieces of a wall, what had once been the corner of a building, partially visible in the ground, covered with grass and weeds.

Moving closer he notices sets of crosses placed at the edges, along a wire fence. Wooden and makeshift, around the periphery of an invisble square. Offerings. Leaning against the fence, he could see a prominent construction sign. He got closer to read it.

The sign was hand painted, but badly faded and peeling; nailed onto the top was a wooden cross:

> **In honor of the civilians and indigenous population that once lived and flourished here, this site is recognized by the missionaries of the Church of the Innocents on this holy day, 3 May, 1987.**
>
> **On September 29, 1982, twenty-seven inhabitants of this village were murdered by the Guatemalan Army. Their surviving were forced to flee and the village was destroyed.**
>
> **Thanks to the efforts of the Central American Youth Relief and the Church of the Innocents to help recognize and honor this site.**

Of all things, it reminded Harry of the times Basher had said in a letter, *You'll be reading about this in the papers before you get this in the mail.*

It was as if to be here was to be in his presence again. Or, almost.

The sun broke the clouds and burned bright through the line of trees, glaring on the sign a blinding yellow. The glare so strong it hurt his eyes. He closed them.

The film hinged an entire life on its final moment captured in all its ingloriousness. Death was not meant to be a spectacle. Death was a private moment to be stifled under blankets, in pure oxygen, without pain, behind closed doors, with loved ones in mind, if not gathered respectfully around. Not like the emotional full out release of the breaking dam, the uncontrollable act of God. The insult of spectacle put the lie to a life of deeds. The cameras magnified the spectacle. This is what happened to Basher, everything that was good about him was somehow tragically emphasized in those shots to his body. Giving vengeful retractors their unspoken vindication. The life humiliatingly memorialized in the bleeding, effusive color of 26 seconds of 8-mm Kodachrome II Safety Film. Playing years later, it seemed somehow, live. By the time the Rasmussen film had entered the collective memory, the insult of its ceremony was the property of pop culture. In the media saturated eighties, nineties and oughts—this piece of celluloid became one more artifact of an era, so produced and reproduced and ubiquitous that somewhere in the world at any time, that 26 seconds of film was being viewed by *someone*.

Harry feels it like a memory.

For Basher, professional calm was a default mode so as to stay on top and not take the drama in, not too quickly or heavily, to find the characteristic image and get away clean. Just another day's work then, the usual odd and slow burn of time, waiting, tempered with an optimism that might not have matched the daily intake of pointless battles, visions of blood, dirt and wrack, the unscripted, noise corrupted world. Except that he couldn't always help himself.

The video: a lazy pan, verite, wide angles of a blazing sun soaked haze over the trees, well into the final minutes, a Western evening sky, unidentified figures on the fringe, evidence of more witnesses who ran for cover when the shots went off. Basher's barest gesture, scolding, entreating, the hand raised to pause, to question. Or it was the open palm up in surrender, not entirely clear, cryptic in a glint of phosphor, bullets like gashes across the stock.

Fallen into a crack in the earth.

Harry is dulled with the images and can replay the half minute spectacle of Basher's death at will. Each colored, fluttering frame carries the burden of that life. Remarkable, how he had memorized it in the hope of redeeming it from this half-minute ignominy. He had come to know the images well, and nothing of the purveyor, the man behind the camera, whose project, ironically, had been shelved in the quarter century interim. Harry bought the stock, or a facsimile thereof, but by that time it had already premiered and likely been forgotten in a million homes during a televised news broadcast. Forgotten in light of the millions of other tragic events of the day, of the year, of the world.

Not so for Harry. He held onto the physical place, touching the earth, lifting off the ground, at the lip of the earth, hanging on and flinching from the heat; through everyone's curious and doubtful looks, the questions of his sanity, trying to keep the lid on. Trying to feel in control of an ever disappearing corner of his well-being, almost letting go, waiting to fall, to cast a final glance backward at a diminishing earth.

## Acknowledgements

Thanks to Goddard College and my advisors Carla Harryman and Douglas A. Martin, and to the MFA program director, Paul Selig; Rebecca Walker and Chris Abani for timely encouragement in Chiang Mai, and Nancy Gerbault; all the editors and publishers who have generously welcomed my writing; the castle writers: Kathy Ahn, Brian Bernbaum, Joe Gelman, and Tim Kinney. Thanks also to all of my friends and family for their support, and especially to Tiff and Simone.

www.ingramcontent.com/pod-product-compliance
Lightning Source LLC
LaVergne TN
LVHW011815060526
838200LV00053B/3786